WRITERS WORKSHOP
OF SCIENCE FICTION & FANTASY

Edited by Bram Stoker Award-winner
MICHAEL KNOST

SEVENTH STAR PRESS

Cover art: Matthew Perry
Illustrations in this book copyright © 2013 Bonnie Wasson,
Matthew Perry, and Seventh Star Press, LLC.

Editor: Michael Knost

Published by Seventh Star Press, LLC.

ISBN Number 978-1-937929-61-9

Seventh Star Press
www.seventhstarpress.com
info@seventhstarpress.com

Printed in the United States of America

First Edition

PERMISSIONS

ACKNOWLEDGEMENTS

I want to offer my sincere appreciation for those who helped make *Writers Workshop of Science Fiction & Fantasy* a reality:

The contributors, without whom this book would offer very little.

Stephen Zimmer and the entire crew at Seventh Star Press for not only believing in this project, but for thinking outside the box and delivering exactly what you promised... and more.

Geoff Fuller, as far as I am concerned, is the best proofreader/editor in the business. Thanks for making me look good... again.

Matt Perry for the incredible cover art and design, and for the great formatting. Thanks for making me look good, too.

Lou Anders for sage advice.

Matt Perry and Bonnie Wasson for such gorgeous art pieces.

Jackie Gamber and the talented folks of Alltrope Media. Your book trailers are nothing short of works of art!

G. Cameron Fuller, Jennifer Collins, F. Keith Davis, Brian J. Hatcher, Frank Larnerd, and hundreds of other friends who had to listen to me talk endlessly about this project.

Last, but certainly not least, everyone who participated in the Kickstarter!

CONTENTS

HONOR ROLL FOR WRITERS WORKSHOP

Seventh Star Press would like to thank and acknowledge several wonderful individuals whose strong support of this project helped to make it a reality.

Isobel A

AT Alexander

Jarod K. and Leslie J. Anderson

James M. Barton

Karen M. Bence

AN Bengco

R. K. Bentley

Garrett Bleakley

Ryan E. Bowe, GISP

Laura Boyd

Jennifer Brozek

Alex R. Carvalho

Christopher Contorno

K+J Fulmer

Andreia Gaita

Azra (Azzypantz) Gani

Elizabeth Gaucher

Gary Greco

Mark Greenberg

Kristján Már Gunnarsson

Dimitri Halkidis

Pádraic D. Hallinan

Hectaimon

Robert Holda

J.D. Hovland

Vicki Hsu

Jochen

Eugene Johnson

Scotty & Will Johnstone

Heather "Talonn" Jones

John Justus

Richard K. Kim

Yvonne Law

Jessica Lay

Fred Leggett

Ryan Litwin

Rebecca McClannahan

Phillip McCollum

J. Miles

Kriss Morton of Cabin Goddess Reviews

Jussi Myllyluoma

Rikard Kro Neckarski

Shawn Polka

Linda Rendell-Hayes

Denise Ritchie

George Selembo

Joe Sergi

Caleb J Smith

Michael J. Sprague

Sean & Stephanie

Lee Eguia Elam Stone

Zbig Strycharz

John N Tobias III

Philippe Tremblay

KT Wagner

Matthew Wasiak

David G. Whaley, Jr.

Bradley G. Wherry

Janice Phelps Williams

Shan Winslow

Kaila Yee

INTRODUCTION

BY MICHAEL KNOST

When I put together *Writers Workshop of Horror* (Woodland Press, 2009) a few years ago, my goal was to produce a writing book I wish would have been available when I began my writing journey. That's why I included a wide variety of pieces focused on specific elements of the craft by writers I felt excelled in the elements I chose for them. The book became an instant hit and continues to sell quite well.

However, *Writers Workshop of Horror* did not address dozens of subjects I was still interested in exploring. By confining the project to the horror genre, I restricted myself from a broader scope of elements and ideas. Since I cut my literary teeth on science fiction and fantasy, I decided to move ahead with a similar project in these fields.

I want you to have a clear understating as to what this book is. *Writers Workshop of Science Fiction & Fantasy* is a collection of essays and interviews by and with many of the movers-and-shakers in the industry. You're going to find varying perspectives and viewpoints, which is why you may find differing opinions on any particular subject.

This is, after all, a collection of advice from professional storytellers. And no two writers have made it to the stage via the same journey—each has made his or her own path to success. And that's one of the strengths of this book, I think. The reader is afforded the luxury of discovering various approaches and then is allowed to choose what works best for him or her.

But what about the rules? How can there be different approaches when there are rules to follow? Besides, we've noticed that the big-name writers we love and respect are breaking the rules!

Here's my advice: use the rules until you break them.

I know that sounds like something from an Abbot and Costello routine, but it's the truth. Use the rules until you break them.

To be honest, there are only two rules you should never break—they just so happen to be rules regarding breaking rules—and I made them up, so take them for what they're worth.

1. Never break a rule unless you know you are breaking a rule.
2. Always have a reason for breaking a rule.

If you know you are breaking a rule, that simply means you have studied the craft enough to understand its *purpose*. When you understand the rule's purpose, yet have a good reason to ignore it, breaking the rule is possibly the best thing you can do.

There's a difference in effect between a rule broken out of ignorance and one broken for a reason. For example, Picasso learned to do masterful realistic sketches before venturing into cubism. James Joyce wrote stunning short stories before wandering into Ulysses. Both of these artists mastered their respective craft by paying close attention to the foundational elements. Once they mastered the fundamentals, they were then ready to create art that was unique to their own talents and most celebrated.

I also want to point out that the reader needn't be a writer of science fiction or fantasy to benefit from the advice in these pages. Writing is writing, and the guidance you'll find here will be just as solid or sound if you apply it to the romance, western, or thriller genres. However, writers of speculative fiction will obviously glean a greater return because the contributors are masters in the same fields.

One more thing I want to point out. Style and voice may not be the only things you find unique to each writer and/or piece. You will also find structure and other little tidbits that are just as distinctive. The works of British contributors will retain British spelling, grammar, and punctuation. However, I designated a universal structure with the interviews to minimize confusion, yet allowed individual liberties in content.

You should be commended for your interest in learning more about the craft. Because you want your writing to improve—it will. Just don't give up.

Don't give up and write every day.

Michael Knost
January 28, 2013

NEIL GAIMAN

WHERE DO YOU GET YOUR IDEAS?

Neil Gaiman writes short fiction, novels, comic books, graphic novels, audio theatre, and films. His notable works include the comic book series *The Sandman* and novels *Stardust, American Gods, Coraline,* and *The Graveyard Book.* Gaiman's writing has won numerous awards, including Hugo, Nebula, and Bram Stoker, as well as the 2009 Newbery Medal and 2010 Carnegie Medal in Literature. He is the first author to win both the Newbery and the Carnegie medals for the same work.

Every profession has its pitfalls. Doctors, for example, are always being asked for free medical advice, lawyers are asked for legal information, morticians are told how interesting a profession that must be and then people change the subject fast. And writers are asked where we get our ideas from.

In the beginning, I used to tell people the not very funny answers, the flip ones: 'From the Idea-of-the-Month Club,' I'd say, or 'From a little ideas shop in Bognor Regis,' 'From a dusty old book full of ideas in my basement,' or even 'From Pete Atkins.' (The last is slightly esoteric, and may need a little explanation. Pete Atkins is a screenwriter and novelist friend of mine, and we decided a while ago that when asked, I would say that I got them from him, and he'd say he got them from me. It seemed to make sense at the time.)

Then I got tired of the not very funny answers, and these days I tell people the truth:

'I make them up,' I tell them. 'Out of my head.'

People don't like this answer. I don't know why not. They look unhappy, as if I'm trying to slip a fast one past them. As if there's a huge secret, and, for reasons of my own, I'm not telling them how it's done.

And of course I'm not. Firstly, I don't know myself where the ideas really come from, what makes them come, or whether one day they'll stop. Secondly, I doubt anyone who asks really wants a three-hour lecture on the creative process. And thirdly, the ideas aren't that important. Really they aren't. Everyone's got an idea for a book, a movie, a story, a TV series.

Every published writer has had it—the people who come up to you and tell you that they've Got An Idea. And boy, is it a Doozy. It's such a Doozy that they want to Cut You In On It. The proposal is always the same—they'll tell you the Idea (the hard bit), you write it down and turn it into a novel (the easy bit), the two of you can split the money fifty-fifty.

I'm reasonably gracious with these people. I tell them, truly, that I have far too many ideas for things as it is, and far too little time. And I wish them the best of luck.

The Ideas aren't the hard bit. They're a small component of the whole. Creating believable people who do more or less what you tell them to is much harder. And hardest by far is the process of simply sitting down and putting one word after another to construct whatever it is you're trying to build: making it interesting, making it new.

But still, it's the question people want to know. In my case, they also want to know if I get them from my dreams. (Answer:

no. Dream logic isn't story logic. Transcribe a dream, and you'll see. Or better yet, tell someone an important dream - 'Well, I was in this house that was also my old school, and there was this nurse and she was really an old witch and then she went away but there was a leaf and I couldn't look at it and I knew if I touched it then something dreadful would happen...' - and watch their eyes glaze over.) And I don't give straight answers. Until recently.

My daughter Holly, who was seven years of age at the time, persuaded me to come in to give a talk to her class. Her teacher was really enthusiastic ('The children have all been making their own books recently, so perhaps you could come along and tell them about being a professional writer. And lots of little stories. They like the stories.') and in I came.

They sat on the floor, I had a chair, fifty seven-year-old-eyes gazed up at me. 'When I was your age, people told me not to make things up,' I told them. 'These days, they give me money for it.' For twenty minutes I talked, then they asked questions.

And eventually one of them asked it.

'Where do you get your ideas?'

And I realized I owed them an answer. They weren't old enough to know any better. And it's a perfectly reasonable question, if you aren't asked it weekly.

This is what I told them:

You get ideas from daydreaming. You get ideas from being bored. You get ideas all the time. The only difference between writers and other people is we notice when we're doing it.

You get ideas when you ask yourself simple questions. The most important of the questions is just, What if...?

(What if you woke up with wings? What if your sister turned into a mouse? What if you all found out that your teacher was

3

planning to eat one of you at the end of term—but you didn't know who?)

Another important question is, If only...

(If only real life was like it is in Hollywood musicals. If only I could shrink myself small as a button. If only a ghost would do my homework.)

And then there are the others: I wonder... ('I wonder what she does when she's alone...') and If This Goes On... ('If this goes on, telephones are going to start talking to each other and cut out the middleman...') and Wouldn't it be interesting if... ('Wouldn't it be interesting if the world used to be ruled by cats?')...

Those questions, and others like them, and the questions they, in their turn, pose ('Well, if cats used to rule the world, why don't they any more? And how do they feel about that?') are one of the places ideas come from.

An idea doesn't have to be a plot notion, just a place to begin creating. Plots often generate themselves when one begins to ask oneself questions about whatever the starting point is.

Sometimes an idea is a person ('There's a boy who wants to know about magic'). Sometimes it's a place ('There's a castle at the end of time, which is the only place there is...'). Sometimes it's an image ('A woman, sitting in a dark room filled with empty faces').

Often ideas come from two things coming together that haven't come together before. ('If a person bitten by a werewolf turns into a wolf what would happen if a goldfish was bitten by a werewolf? What would happen if a chair was bitten by a werewolf?')

All fiction is a process of imagining: whatever you write, in whatever genre or medium, your task is to make things up convincingly and interestingly and new.

And when you've an idea—which is, after all, merely something to hold on to as you begin—what then?

My idea of hell is a blank sheet

My idea of hell is a blank
sheet of paper.

staring at it,

of a sin

been to   black

glek

charac

tory than

besn   before?

Well, then you write. You put one word after another until it's finished—whatever it is.

Sometimes it won't work, or not in the way you first imagined. Sometimes it doesn't work at all. Sometimes you throw it out and start again.

I remember, some years ago, coming up with a perfect idea for a Sandman story. It was about a succubus who gave writers and artists and songwriters ideas in exchange for some of their lives. I called it Sex and Violets.

It seemed a straightforward story, and it was only when I came to write it I discovered it was like trying to hold fine sand: every time I thought I'd got hold of it, it would trickle through my fingers and vanish.

I wrote at the time:

I've started this story twice, now, and got about halfway through it each time, only to watch it die on the screen.

Sandman is, occasionally, a horror comic. But nothing I've written for it has ever gotten under my skin like this story I'm now going to have to wind up abandoning (with the deadline already a thing of the past). Probably because it cuts so close to home. It's the ideas—and the ability to put them down on paper, and turn them into stories—that make me a writer. That mean I don't have to get up early in the morning and sit on a train with people I don't know, going to a job I despise.

My idea of hell is a blank sheet of paper. Or a blank screen. And me, staring at it, unable to think of a single thing worth saying, a single character that people could believe in, a single story that hasn't been told before.

Staring at a blank sheet of paper.

Forever.

I wrote my way out of it, though. I got desperate (that's another flip and true answer I give to the where-do-you-get-your-ideas question. 'Desperation.' It's up there with 'Boredom' and 'Deadlines'. All these answers are true to a point.) and took my own terror, and the core idea, and crafted a story called Calliope, which explains, I think pretty definitively, where writers get their ideas from. It's in a book called *Dream Country*. You can read it if you like. And, somewhere in the writing of that story, I stopped being scared of the ideas going away.

Where do I get my ideas from?

I make them up.

Out of my head.

LOU ANDERS

NEBULOUS MATTERS, OR
SPECULATIONS ON SUBGENRE

Lou Anders is the Hugo Award-winning editorial director
of the SF&F imprint Pyr, a Chesley Award-winning art
director, and the editor of nine anthologies. He has also
been nominated for five additional Hugos, four additional
Chesleys, as well as the Philip K. Dick, Locus, Shirley
Jackson, and three WFC Awards. Visit him online at www.
louanders.com, on Twitter @LouAnders, and on Facebook.

Sometimes I think that subgenres were invented for no other
reason than to give speculative fiction fans something to argue
about. Author Damon Knight once famously said, "Science fiction
is what we point to when we say 'science fiction.'" There are other
definitions I prefer, but I think the larger point is that definitions
aren't definitive.

A wise person once said that genre (and by extension subgenre)
definitions should be descriptive not prescriptive. It's very easy
to identify the middle of a subgenre, but very dangerous to draw
fences at the borders. Or, to put it another way, it's easy to proclaim
you're there when you stand on the top of the mountain, but when
you climb down into the valley, it's a lot harder to identify the
exact point where the mountain you were on ends and the next
mountain over starts.

Which is not to say that subgenres don't serve a function beyond the rather obvious function of giving us something to argue about online and in bars. Genre categories exist for a very good reason—to allow readers who enjoy a thing to be able to find more of it. Genres and subgenres are signifiers that help readers connect with books the way different-colored flowers attract different kinds of insects. In the broadest sense, they are a way of saying, "This is the sort of thing you'll like, if you like this sort of thing."

To begin with (because I continually meet people who do not know the word), I should explain that the term *genre* itself is a term for a category of literature. When we speak of the speculative fiction genre, we are using an umbrella term for many varieties of imaginative literature, including science fiction, fantasy, and horror. Within these broad genres, we have myriad subgenres. And, it is important to note, genre and subgenre are fluid, shifting things. What comprises a subgenre today may not be the same as what is said to comprise it tomorrow.

But speaking generally, let's look at a few.

Science fiction is often said to be the literature of ideas, though, rather recently, Elizabeth Bear proclaimed that it was the literature of testing ideas to the breaking point, and I rather like that distinction. "The literature of ideas" may place an undue importance on novelty, whereas the concept of testing (and by extension retesting) ideas gets closer to the genre's point. Generally speaking, science fiction can serve a number of important functions. It can be prediction, as in the literature of H.G. Wells and Jules Verne. It can be inspirational, in the way it inspires actual scientists and inventors. It can be cautionary, in an "if this goes on" sort of way, as in *Brave New World* or *1984*. And it can be satirical, a "fun house mirror" held up to the present (as Paolo Bacigalupi says), a way of understanding ourselves by approaching the now from an oblique angle. All of these functions are important and relevant, and it is a losing game to try and determine which is the most important and most relevant. So we won't! But within science fiction, we have a tradition of many subgenres, with new ones emerging all the time.

Hard science fiction is a term for those works of science fiction that emphasize technical details of the narrative and/or strive for a high degree of scientific accuracy in the depiction of the science of the story. Hard science fiction authors can present stories in which the physics and mathematics of a tale are front and center, as in the work of Greg Egan and Neal Stephenson. Some apply rigorously detailed rules to the workings of their invented technologies—such as complex explanations for nonexistent technologies like faster-than-light travel (FTL), while others feel that truly "hard" hard science fiction must stick only to those technologies deemed possible in light of the current understanding of scientific and technical knowledge. Larry Niven's *Ringworld* is a classic example of hard science fiction, as is Greg Egan's *Schild's Ladder*. A recent offshoot of hard science fiction, perhaps a subgenre in its own right but more accurately labeled a movement, is *mundane science fiction*. Inspired by an idea of computer programmer Julian Todd, and founded by novelist Geoff Ryman, the mundane science fiction movement forgoes the use of such science fiction tropes as FTL, teleportation, wormholes, and contact with alien species, dismissing these as "wish fulfillment fantasies" and choosing to focus instead on the Earth, the solar system, and only those sciences and technologies that are accurate in our current understanding. What separates mundane science fiction from hard science fiction is this idea that the nonscientifically accurate offerings of the science fiction genre are unprofitable, potentially damaging pursuits.

Soft science fiction is not as easily defined as hard science fiction. Some readers and critics consider soft science fiction to be "fuzzy science" science fiction and would include any story that included "impossible" technologies like FTL to be soft. However, the more popular definition of soft science fiction is that it is the literature of the genre most concerned with character, ideas, and social sciences, rather than with the engineering and technical aspects of world building. In either regard, Jules Verne would be seen as a practitioner of hard science fiction whereas H.G. Wells would be seen as predominantly soft. Ursula K. Le Guin's *The Left Hand of Darkness* is one of the most famous examples of this category, but wherever the line is drawn, science fiction undoubtedly produces as much soft work as hard, possibly more.

Fan and author Wilson Tucker coined the term *space opera* in 1941 as a derogative term to describe hackneyed spaceship stories. It was meant to suggest the soap opera and the horse opera (a possibly derogative term for western film). But like so many labels that have outgrown their stigma, space opera generally refers to tales of high adventure, set largely in outer space, and often involving conflicts on an interplanetary, even galactic scale. *Star Wars* is, of course, the most famous example of the form, but the subgenre extends back as far as the formative Lensman series by E.E. "Doc" Smith to the sophisticated, literary work of Iain M. Banks. In fact, a subset of space opera might be said to be the *new space opera*, a recent tradition, largely coming out of the UK, that could be said to be concerned with applying sophisticated literary technique, emphasizing character, and examining social issues to the tropes of the subgenre.

An overlapping subgenre with space opera is *military science fiction*. Military science fiction is exactly what it sounds like, and is that branch of science fiction concerned with large-scale battles and military scenarios. Examples include Robert Heinlein's *Starship Troopers*, Lois McMaster Bujold's Vorkosigan Saga, Joe Haldeman's *The Forever War*, and David Drake's Hammer's Slammers stories. Ironically, despite having the word *war* in the title, a case could be made that *Star Wars* itself is insufficiently military in tone to count in this subgenre. But remember what I said about erecting fences in the valleys.

New Wave science fiction was not a subgenre but a movement, but it is worth discussing here for its influence on the field and its direct inspiration of another subgenre. The new wave was a movement that began in the 1960s and centered around Michael Moorcock in his editorship of *New Worlds* magazine. The thinking was that both science fiction and literary fiction had reached creative dead ends and that both genres could benefit by the crossbreeding of techniques. The new waves were characterized by experimentation, by an emphasis on the soft sciences, on character over ideas, and on a general disdain for a good many science fiction tropes of the past. J.G. Ballard's famous statement that, "the only true alien planet is earth" typifies the ideals of the new wave movement, though it is interesting that one of its practitioners, M. John Harrison, wrote a space opera called *The Centauri Device* that, in its cynical treatment of the subgenre, is seen as the start of the aforementioned new space opera of more sophisticated narratives. The influence of the new wave is felt everywhere in genre today, but is also seen in the emergence, in the mainstream, of authors like Jonathan Lethem, Margaret Atwood, and Michael Chabon.

Cyberpunk is the genre concerned with the intersection of high levels of (computer) technology and street life. Its most famous practitioners are William Gibson, Bruce Sterling, and Pat Cadigan.

The genre is concerned with hackers, artificial intelligence, cyberspace, the Internet, and the digitizing of human consciousness. The emphasis of style and atmosphere recalls something of the earlier new wave movement, and it is arguable that the cyberpunk movement could not have occurred without the new wave movement as precedent. Moreover, there have been attempts to retroactively claim authors like J.G. Ballard and Philip K. Dick as pre-cyberpunk, just as works like John Meaney's *To Hold Infinity* have been described as post-cyberpunk. Cyberpunk's influence is felt in films like *Blade Runner, Strange Days*, and, of course, *The Matrix*, as well as in the iPhone on which you are quite possibly reading this book. Indeed, we have cyberpunk to thank for inspiring a great many computer programmers—it was William Gibson who coined the word *cyberspace*—but also for unfortunately ensuring that every subsequent movement and genre had to have the suffix *punk* tacked on at the end. Thus we have biopunk (biotechnological themes), nanopunk (nanotechnological themes), and steampunk.

Which brings us to a current hot trend, the subgenre (or movement?) of *steampunk*. Steampunk was a term reportedly coined by K.W. Jeter in the late 1980s to describe stories that imitated the conventions of Victorian science fiction. It's defining works were Jeter's *Morlock Night*, Michael Moorcock's *Warlord of the Air*, and William Gibson and Bruce Sterling's *The Difference Engine*, and, later, Paul Di Filippo's 1995 *Steampunk Trilogy*. While there were other works in this subgenre, steampunk remained a minor subgenre within science fiction for many years, while a parallel movement in fashion and art developed almost independently of the literature. This larger steampunk movement has fed back into the literary genre from whence it sprang and has rekindled steampunk and made it one of the hottest subgenres in the current publishing climate. Jess Nevins has summed the movement up succinctly in saying that, "Steampunk is what happens when goths discover brown," and, though flippant, there is some truth in that assessment. Meanwhile, though historically associated most closely with Victoriana, steampunk asthetics spread to other historic periods and locations, giving rise to the *weird west* subgenre (as typified by the television series, *The Wild, Wild West*, and most recently, by Mike Resnick's *The Buntline Special*), clockpunk (typically works dealing with anachronistic technologies in a Renaissance or Renaissance-seeming setting, as in Jay Lake's *Mainspring*), deiselpunk (George Mann's *Ghosts of Manhattan*, the film *Sky Captain and the World of Tomorrow*) and steam fantasy (China Mieville's Bas Lag novels and the Shadows of the Apt series by Adrian Tchaikovsky). At the time of this writing, there seems no end in sight to the popularity of steampunk, either within the speculative fiction genre or outside in the wider culture. But as Charles Fort once said, "A social growth cannot find out the use of steam engines, until comes steam-engine-time."

Turning to science fiction's sibling genre, *fantasy*, we see as much diversity as we do in SF, as well as—as you might expect—considerable overlap.

Epic fantasy, sometimes called *high fantasy*, is the subgenre typically concerned with grand struggles against supernatural threats in an invented (or *secondary*) world. J.R.R. Tolkien's *The Lord of the Rings* is the undisputed exemplar of this form. Epic fantasy is the most popular and commercially successful subgenre in the fantasy field and these days largely dominates not only the other subgenres of fantasy fiction but science fiction as well. Robert Jordan, Terry Brooks, Brandan Sanderson, and George R.R. Martin are a few of its most famous practitioners.

The other half of the fantasy tradition is *sword and sorcery*, a subgenre that has its roots in the pulp magazines of the 1930s and the writings of Robert E. Howard, creator of Conan the Barbarian. Sword and sorcery is generally grittier, more vulgar, and more personal than epic fantasy. It has been described succinctly as "fantasy with dirt" and could also be said to be where fantasy literature intersects with the western. Its protagonists tend to be more self-interested and less heroic, its scale tends to be much smaller in scope, and its morality tends towards gray. Michael Morcock's Elric and Fritz Leiber's Fafhrd and the Gray Mouser are archetypal sword and sorcery characters, their exploits required reading, along with Howard's barbarian. Current sword and sorcery works would include Scott Lynch's Gentleman Bastards series and James Enge's reoccurring character Morlock Ambrosius.

These days, a kind of *sword and sorcery aesthetic* has worked its way into epic fantasy, producing what some call the "new, gritty fantasy" that sees an emphasis on character, politics, the realistic depiction of violence and human nature, and a rejection of less seemingly sophisticated narratives of good verses evil. The Black Company novels of Glen Cook, Steven Erikson's The Malazan Book of the Fallen series, Joe Abercrombie's The First Law trilogy, and George R.R. Martin's A Song of Ice and Fire series are quintessential examples of this new fantasy.

Urban fantasy is the subgenre of fantasy that sees supernatural elements blended with contemporary, urban environments. Originally, urban fantasy would have been a term for works like Harlan Ellison's *Deathbird Stories*, a collection of stories about modern-day deities, John Crowley's *Little, Big*, and the Newford stories of Charles De Lint. Urban fantasy has enjoyed a surge in popularity and something of a transformation in the wake of the

Buffy, the Vampire Slayer television series and the rise of authors like Laurell K. Hamilton (her Anita Blake series) and Jim Butcher (The Dresden Files series). These days, urban fantasy rivals epic fantasy in popularity, and sees a great deal of crossover with its sister genre of *paranormal romance*, itself a subgenre of the romance genre that intersects with speculative fiction. *New York Times* bestselling author Marjorie M. Liu has opined that the difference between urban fantasy and paranormal romance is whether the protagonist ends the book in a functional or dysfunctional relationship. Meanwhile, another overlapping subgenre is *dark fantasy*—the intersection of fantasy and horror.

The last subgenre we'll address—though by no means the last subgenre to emerge—is that of *sci-fantasy*. Sci-fantasy, or *science fantasy*, is the subgenre that mixes elements of science fiction and fantasy together. Works like the *Star Wars* films are often called sci-fantasy in that they borrow the tropes of space opera but without any scientific explanations, real or imagined. But literate works such as Jack Vance's far future Dying Earth stories and Gene Wolfe's Book of the New Sun are also classified as sci-fantasy. Near-future milieus into which magic has returned, such as the Shadowrun role-playing game and Justina Robson's Quantum Gravity series are sci-fantasy, of the urban fantasy variety, while Kay Kenyon's Empire and the Rose quartet is sci-fantasy of the space opera variety, in so far as it takes Sir Arthur C. Clarke's dictum that "any sufficiently advanced science is indistinguishable from magic" seriously in the technological underpinnings of its alien world. Given that the subgenre incorporates space opera of dubious science, tales of elves and dwarves in a contemporary setting, and far future settings with seemingly magical beings, it is obvious this is perhaps the most broad and nebulous subgenre we have explored.

This brings me to my last, and perhaps most important, point. Subgenre classification is as useful as it is fun. If it is helpful, as a writer or a reader, to think in terms of subgenre, by all means do so. But when the definitions morph into constraints and the constraints give rise to heated arguments, it is time to take a breath and step back. As we have seen, all of these descriptors are fluid and ever changing, and all we can say for certain is that the speculative fiction field is a rich and fertile ground to till. May it be ever thus.

LUCY A. SNYDER

URSULA K. LE GUIN TALKS ABOUT A LIFETIME IN THE CRAFT

Lucy A. Snyder is the Bram Stoker Award-winning author of the novels *Spellbent* and *Shotgun Sorceress* and the collections *Sparks and Shadows, Chimeric Machines,* and *Installing Linux on a Dead Badger.* Her writing has appeared in *Strange Horizons, Weird Tales, Hellbound Hearts, Chiaroscuro, Greatest Uncommon Denominator,* and *Lady Churchill's Rosebud Wristlet.* She's a graduate of the Clarion workshop, directs the Context Writing Workshops, and mentors students in Seton Hill University's MFA program in Writing Popular Fiction.

Ursula K. Le Guin is the grande dame of science fiction. Since 1968, she has published twenty-one novels, eleven short story collections, three books of essays, twelve children's books, and six collections of poetry. She has also edited volumes such as *The Norton Book of Science Fiction* (1993) and *Edges: Thirteen New Tales From The Borderlands of the Imagination* (1980). She has won five Hugos, six Nebulas, two World Fantasy Awards, three Tiptree Awards, among others. Le Guin has also been honored with the World Fantasy Lifetime Achievement Award, the SFWA Grand Master Award, and the Science Fiction Research Association Pilgrim Award for her lifetime contributions to SF and fantasy; she is also a Science Fiction Hall of Fame Living Inductee.

Lucy A. Snyder: What is your process for preparing to write? Do you have any routines such as a cup of tea before you start, or do you dive right in? And what tools do you use?

Ursula K. Le Guin: I sit down at the computer or with the notebook and reread what I wrote yesterday, and probably start editing it and rewriting, and then (hopefully) slide on into composing.

I write with a Pilot P-500 pen (getting harder to find) in bound or spiral-bound notebooks when I'm traveling or when I want to sit outside while writing, which I love to do. My computer is always a Mac, currently a MacBook Pro. I compose on it, and the stuff from the notebooks gets fed into it pretty promptly.

Snyder: How have your writing habits changed over the course of your career?

Le Guin: Really not at all, except that when my kids were young I could only write after they went to bed—nine to midnight. I was happy to get back to morning writing when they finally were all off to school. I am not methodical, and I don't make myself write if I have no story in mind, but if I do, I try to make room in the day for it, preferably the morning.

About being unmethodical: I make sure I can be unmethodical—I write on spec. I don't promise work. I don't sell my work, in fact nobody sees it until it's finished. This leaves me freedom. The price is risk. Writing on spec, you can spend months on a piece that never gets published. I've spent years submitting and not selling. But to me, promising unwritten work is locking myself up in a little cell and dropping the key through the food slot. To work, I have to have room. "A room of my own"—not owned by an editor or a publisher. My place.

Snyder: Is there one book that you think all aspiring science fiction writers should read without fail?

Le Guin: Strunk and White's *The Elements of Style*. (Maybe memorize it?)

Snyder: Elsewhere, you've said that you've learned a lot from reading Virginia Woolf. Can you elaborate on some of the writing craft lessons her work has taught you?

Le Guin: I learned that shifting point of view/shifting voice(s) can be an endlessly demanding and fascinating way to tell a story. That plot does not matter to the kind of fiction I like best, but story growing out of relationships is what matters. That if you can't read it out loud with pleasure it isn't really worth reading.

Snyder: What do you find satisfying about writing short stories as opposed to writing novels, and vice versa?

Le Guin: You can do a short story in a day or two—in fact, often you have to, or you lose it. That passion of writing is good. A novel demands a great part of your body, mind, and soul for months. That long-term commitment is good. One of my favorite forms is the novella, which combines the compression of the short story with the spaciousness of the novel. You have room to describe

21

things and to move your characters around in in time and space, but still, the whole thing has got to be moving pretty much in one direction all the time. It's a beautiful size for a story.

Snyder: You've edited several anthologies—was editing a positive experience for you? Did you learn anything from the experience that you brought to bear on your own writing?

Le Guin: I love reading, so I like putting together stories that I particularly liked for other people to discover. I don't think I learned anything about my own writing by anthologizing. Learning how to critique, from teaching workshops and being in writing groups— from that, I am still learning a lot.

Snyder: What has writing poetry done for your own fiction, and vice versa?

Le Guin: I have no idea how my poetry and my fiction interrelate. They don't visibly overlap much. They are very different arts, and I'm lucky to be able to work with both of them.

Snyder: You work very hard and consciously at your craft. Are there any writing forms/styles you'd still like to try that you haven't, or ones that you've tried and feel you have yet to master?

Le Guin: I wish I could write a play! But I haven't the faintest notion of how it's done—I stand in awe—playwriting is a mystery to me and always will be.

Snyder: You've said elsewhere that to you science fiction is a form of realist literature because it's about futures that could happen, but just haven't yet. What's your favorite modern advance that would have seemed science fictional in 1966? Conversely, what event or development has disappointed you by not having happened yet?

Le Guin: Well, it's not exactly a favorite thing; it's more like a giant embarrassment thing: in 1966, who in science fiction (or out of it) foresaw the huge transformation of society by the personal computer and the Internet?

And the biggest disappointment is not something that didn't happen, but something that has just gone on and on happening. When I wrote *The Lathe of Heaven* in 1971, I honestly thought that by 2002 we wouldn't be driving private automobiles—we wouldn't be so idiotic as to keep relying on fossil oil and fouling the world for another thirty years.

Snyder: You've won many literary and genre awards. Which one has meant the most to you, and why?

Le Guin: The first Nebula and Hugo, for *The Left Hand of Darkness*, were milestones to me—validation. They meant readers understood what I was trying to do and liked it. The first story my agent sold to *The New Yorker* was not an award, but it was a comparable reward— an exhilarating breakthrough. Yeah! Green light!

JAMES GUNN

BEGINNINGS

James Gunn is a science fiction author, editor, scholar, and anthologist. His *Road to Science Fiction* collections are considered his most important scholarly books. He won a Hugo Award for a nonfiction book in 1983 for *Isaac Asimov: The Foundations of Science Fiction*. He has been named the 2007 Damon Knight Memorial Grand Master by the Science Fiction and Fantasy Writers of America. He is a professor emeritus of English, and the Director of the Center for the Study of Science Fiction, both at the University of Kansas.

There's nothing like a good beginning—unless it's a good ending. But, as I used to tell my fiction-writing students, without a good beginning the reader will never get to the ending.

That opening sentence better grab the reader. I'm not talking about the *narrative hook* that used to be touted by the old pulp writers—though it's not to be scorned just because it is hackneyed—but the needs of the science fiction story to propel the reader into a different world. Theodore Sturgeon, the quintessential science fiction short story writer, and Don Ward, the long-time editor of *Zane Grey's Western Magazine*, once collaborated on a series of western stories. They challenged each other to a contest for the best opening sentence. Ted's was "At last they sat a dance out," but Ted conceded that Don's was better: "They banged out through the cabin door and squared off in the snow outside."

The advice to apprentice western story writers was "shoot the sheriff in the first paragraph." That was to provide an opportunity for everybody to compete for dominance as well as to establish that the issue was life-and-death. In science fiction the challenge is to alert the reader to what is different about the world of the story and, if possible, to plant a clue that will eventually combine with other clues to complete the jigsaw puzzle that is the alternate reality.

In the early 1960s I attended a Westercon in Santa Barbara at which A. E. van Vogt gave a talk about his writing methods. Van Vogt was the master of what I called, in volume three of my *The Road to Science Fiction* anthologies, "fairy tales of science." He wrote a seminal essay for Lloyd Eshbach's 1947 *Of Worlds Beyond* on "Complication in the Science Fiction Story" (James Blish called Van Vogt's technique "the extensively recomplicated plot") in which he recommended writing in 800-word scenes and throwing into each scene whatever new idea he had in his head. It made for exciting if not always fully comprehensible narrative. But then Van Vogt's methods were unique; in Santa Barbara, for instance, he described how when he went to sleep with a story problem he always awakened with the solution, so he set his alarm to wake him every two hours so that he could write down the ideas that were fresh out of his dreams. But he went on to say that he had focused on writing what he called "the science fiction sentence."

He didn't explain what a "science fiction sentence" was, so I've come up with my own definition. A science fiction sentence is a statement that isn't true in our world but is true in the science fiction world at hand. An example is the opening sentence of Philip José Farmer's "Sail On! Sail On!": "Friar Sparks sat wedged between the wall and the realizer." The reason this is a science fiction sentence is that there is no "realizer" in our world (and maybe no "Friar Sparks" either), but there is in the "Sail On! Sail On!" world. That world is the first voyage of Christopher Columbus, but in an alternate history in which Friar Bacon was embraced by the Catholic Church, instead of being excommunicated, and his scientific concerns adopted by a monastic order, so that there is a radio on the first voyage and a primitive electric light. There's more to the story than that, but it's that first sentence we're inspecting and its work at creating a new world for the reader.

Poul Anderson once said that what readers wanted from fiction were the twin pleasures of surprise and rightness. The end of the story ought to come out in a way the reader doesn't expect, but the rationale for it ought to be apparent on re-reading. The reader ought to say, "My God! How surprising. But I should have seen it coming." Though that applies to endings, it applies even more to beginnings where the clues are planted that will lead inevitably, though not obviously, to the ending.

In the late 1950s I took a writers workshop from Caroline Gordon (one of the Southern expatriates along with husband Allen Tate and Robert Penn Warren). It was my first exposure to theories of writing and I learned a lot. One of Gordon's rules was that the ending of a story should be implicit in the first paragraph. One of my favorite examples of that rule was the opening sentence of Ernest Hemingway's "The Old Man and the Sea": "He was an old man who fished alone in a skiff in the Gulf Stream and he had gone eighty-four days now without catching a fish."

A good example of that in science fiction is the opening paragraph of Alfred Bester's "Fondly Fahrenheit": "He doesn't know which of us I am these days, but they know one truth. You must own nothing but yourself. You must make your own life, live your own life, and die your own death ... or else you will die another's." Or Frederik Pohl's "Day Million": "On this day I want to tell you about, which will be about a thousand years from now, there were a boy, a girl and a love story. Now, although I haven't said much so far, none of it is true."

Novels, I should insert here, are a different genre. Readers have more patience with novels, knowing that they're settled in for the long haul and willing to let the process play out at a more leisurely pace. There are, to be sure, famous opening sentences, like Dickens's *A Tale of Two Cities*, "It was the best of times; it was the worst of times." But like DuMaurier's "Last night I dreamt I went to Manderly again" from *Rebecca*, the lines are more famous for their contexts than their effectiveness. Or infamous, like Bulwer-Lytton's "It was a dark and stormy night." One of my favorites, though, from Raphael Sabbatini's *Scaramouche*, was, "He was born with the gift of laughter and a sense that the world was mad."

The short story has to work more quickly.

It also has to get into the story quicker. One of the major problems of inexperienced writers is to start their stories slowly, like a broad jumper begins his runway approach to the pit. Some experts call it "walking to the story." Isaac Asimov came every week to visit *Astounding Science Fiction/Analog* editor John W. Campbell to discuss his story ideas. On one such occasion he proposed a robot story incorporating religion. But on his next visit he told Campbell that he had run into problems writing what turned out to be "Reason," the second robot story and the story from which his three laws of robotics were derived. Campbell told him that when it happened to him he had started the story too soon. Asimov took that advice and started "Reason" one week after his two engineers had assembled the robot QT-1—"Cutie"—and were trying to respond to his disbelief.

When I was writing plays back in my undergraduate days, a professor gave me a book on playwriting that contained the advice: throw away the first act. Fiction writing textbooks have recommended something similar—that a novelist should throw away the first chapter and a short-story writer, the first scene. All those, the experts say, are written for the author's benefit, to get him or her started. The audience or the reader don't need them.

Many years ago I ran across a story in *The Saturday Evening Post* or *Collier's* (that dates it!) that started with the sentence, "A story, like a puppy, should be picked up a little ahead of the middle." Generally speaking—all such admonitions have their exceptions—a story should be started when the story issue is engaged. In "Reason" the issue is Cutie's refusal to believe that Powell and Donovan, the comparatively feeble and mentally deficient humans, have created him and continues with their failures to convince the robot otherwise. The reader should be thrown into the middle of the situation, where the tension is high and the issues are engaged. After that, background information—exposition—can be filled in as necessary. And it often isn't necessary. My definition of exposition is information the author wants to provide the reader that the reader doesn't want to read. Once questions have been raised in the reader's mind, exposition loses its curse by becoming answers that the reader wants. Giving the reader incentives makes all the difference.

The Kuttners, Henry and his wife C. L. Moore, were masters of this art. The masterfully constructed "Private Eye" begins with a killing in a metropolitan business office. Two men are seen arguing. One picks up an ornamental whip and strikes the other with it, who grabs an ornamental knife off the desk and kills his attacker. The story shifts to two men who are watching this occur in front of their eyes! Only then do the Kuttners tell us that devices have been invented that read the impressions light waves make on the walls around them. Now that motives can be traced, only premeditated murders are punished. The rest of the story is about the way in which unpunishable murder can be committed in such a system, like Alfred Bester's concept in *The Demolished Man* of how someone can get away with murder in a telepathic society. Bester, too, starts with the murder in the first chapter (as well as the guilt). But in both cases the involving action occurs before the explanation of the situation in which it makes sense, and the explanation is received by the reader as engrossing answers to the questions raised by the opening scene or chapter. Or, better yet, a writer can omit the explanations and allow the actions of the story to speak for themselves: show, don't tell. A well-crafted story is like a stage play in which the reader—the audience—provides interpretation for what goes on, and the author withholds his authorial voice.

Beginnings also are the place in which the questions are raised that the story intends to answer, and avoids or answers immediately the questions it does not intend to answer. Control of the reader's expectations is the key to a successful story. Sometimes the question is a simple "what happens next?" Other times the question is "why is the character doing that?" Or "how is the character going to get out of that predicament?" At its most subtle, the question may be "why is the story being told this way?" Or why are the characters behaving this way. Or even "why does the story use this kind of diction or this kind of sentence structure?"

Stories that frustrate us are often those that don't raise the right questions or don't answer the questions they raise. Or they raise questions that conflict with each other, like a story of character told in the diction of an action story, or, more often, the other way around: an action story told in the diction of someone's internal conflict. And yet a combination of approaches often elicits a better response from the story and the reader—often a flawed hero helps to ground the story in the real world and to elicit reader sympathy rather than admiration, and thus deeper involvement. An action story involving an introspective protagonist and told in a diction appropriate to that introspection can elevate a formula story into a narrative that seems far more believable or more challenging, like Michael Bishop's "Rogue Tomato," whose elevated diction contrasts with his protagonist's working class origins. It also starts with an effective opening (with some tributes to Kafka and Philip K. Dick): "When Philip K. awoke, he found that overnight he had grown from a reasonably well shaped, bilaterally symmetrical human being into... a rotund and limbless body circling a gigantic, gauzy red star. In fact, by the simple feel, by the total aura projected into the seeds of his consciousness, Philip K. concluded that he was a tomato. A tomato of approximately the same dimensions and mass as the planet Mars."

One good way to come up with good story ideas is to change one or more elements in a traditional theme, take a new look at it, and come up with a more satisfying response. That is something Canada's Robert Sawyer, whose novel *Flashforward* has been dramatized as a recent television series, has made a career of.

All that is not to say, either, that reader expectations must always be satisfied. Sometimes the joy of reading is the disappointed expectation, or the story that arouses a generic response only to demonstrate, usually with a more sophisticated development, that the generic response is a cliché that should be exposed and that the more realistic response is superior. That is the reason, for instance, that some writers evoke a fantasy response to a story that is going to resolve itself as science fiction, as in Robert Silverberg's *The*

Kingdoms of the Wall in which a quest through hidden dangers leads to a revelation at the top of the mountain. Or Michael Swanwick's *The Iron-Dragon's Daughter,* which begins in a Dickensian workshop in a fantasy land and later reveals that the young protagonist has been abducted from our reality. Or sometimes when they evoke a science fiction response to a story that is going to resolve itself as fantasy, as in Swanwick's *Stations of the Tide.* And it may be the reason why the New Weird, as evidenced in China Miéville's *Perdido Street Station,* achieves its special effect by offering a mixture of fantasy and science fiction, or fantasy told with realistic details and back story. Sometimes an author can use the protocols for reading genres to achieve other effects that expand the genre or its capabilities.

Finally, a well-crafted beginning provides instructions for the reader, first identifying the genre, then establishing the mood and preparing the reader to laugh or weep, to hold his breath or chill his blood, to anticipate the success of the characters in solving their problems or accomplishing their ends or developing the character or the will or the ability to enable their decisive actions, or to dread their failure. Unless it doesn't and the author decides to approximate the complexities and ambiguities of real life—to show, in Hemingway's term, "the way it was."

I admire the writers who can get away with that. Sometimes it works. Often it doesn't. Sometimes it works for some readers and not for all, and maybe not for most. The only thing a writer can always depend upon is craft. Craft doesn't always enable the author to scale mountains. That depends upon the author's talent and inspiration and dedication. But craft is like the mountaineer's tools and experience. They help when the going gets tough.

GEORGE ZEBROWSKI

MIDDLES

George Zebrowski is an author and editor who has written and edited a number of books. He lives with author Pamela Sargent, with whom he has co-written a number of books, including *Star Trek* novels. He won the John W. Campbell Memorial Award in 1999 for his novel *Brute Orbits*. Three of his short stories, "Heathen God," "The Eichmann Variations," and "Wound the Wind" have been nominated for the Nebula Award, and "The Idea Trap" was nominated for the Theodore Sturgeon Award.

Let's get right into the middle of it, *in medias res*, in the time-honored tradition of Homer's story of *The Odyssey*, which starts at a point of intriguing interest, then fills in the backstory as it moves ahead to the highest point of the drama and its denouement. I use the reference as a narrative hook (there are other ways to begin) on the way to story *middles* and to make a point about the fatality of beginnings in the writing of fiction.

Openings are fun. Endings are harder but even more fun when you leap to them without doing all the middle work, which you have to do to find the honest ending for your story rather than simply impose something; to discover that ending you have to go through the middle.

Middles that justify the openings and *earn* the endings are the hardest to develop. That is why most stories, even very good ones, have something wrong with their middles, but good writers conceal this flaw, hoping that the reader will simply accept that the author wants to get on with it, past the sag that heft in the middle might bring. Such seemingly slimmer stories can stand up to one or two readings, but maybe not to careful study; those that can are the classics.

The middle develops the promise of the opening, leads into the drama, and *earns* the ending. Without the middle of a story or novel, there is not much of a story, only the conclusion to an argument that is not much different from the premise: a house built from the roof down simply will not stand. You may have guessed the ending, but how do you get there? The answer is through the middle, which might well carry more interest than any ending.

You can mix up the opening, middle, and end, but neither the writer or reader must mistake them; you must know which is which or the story won't hold together—it may even be incomprehensible. As a writer you must know what you are doing and when, and you must know when you succeed and when you fail. You can't just insist to yourself that you know the success or failure of what you have written; you must be able to prove it to yourself and convince others. That means constant rereading. If you can't reread it five times, how can you expect an editor, much less a reader, to read it merely once?

Fun openings come to writers all the time, especially to full-time professionals, whose ulterior motives of earnings and accomplishment (the second is the better motive) drive them. Openings are like being washed up on a shore with nowhere to go. By all means write them down, and then face up to the unknown territory that is the middle. In a novel it's a whole continent of discovery, more to be found than invented, perhaps even inexhaustible except through the dramatic decisions that lead to one possible outcome. In a short story it's a sprint, but you don't know how fast you'll need to run it. Maybe you'll just have to walk it through the first time, then adjust the pace in later drafts.

I have one favorite opening, for which I may never find a middle or an end. Maybe it'll just stay as a bit of poetry, also incomplete:

> *My cat's teeth are capped with silver. Together we hunt werewolves.*

What's the middle of this one? Where does it take place? This one is not the kind of story that comes to you all at once, as exposition, development, drama, and denouement. Example:

- A man lived in France. (exposition)
- He hated his wife. (development)
- "Take that!" he shouted, stabbing her. (drama)
- He's exposed and the police chase him. (more drama)
- Police catch him. "I hated her," he says, "and I'm not sorry." (denouement)

As Frank O'Connor, the great short story writer and teacher, has pointed out, the drama, the heart of a story begins when the chorus (author) stops talking and the characters take over to do what they have to do to be who they are; to do that you have to discover the truth about them and get it to the reader. O'Connor gives as an example a story that is nearly all middle—"Hills Like White Elephants" by Ernest Hemingway, in which all exposition and development is cut to the bone and included in the middle, as is the ending—thus telling us that the drama, the middle, is everything of real interest. Kurt Vonnegut says start the story as close to the end as possible, and maybe Hemingway took it all too far, but the story works, especially upon rereading; it is a great example of how technique in the short story has evolved from more expansive ways while holding us with the drama. You can write in more expansive ways, but be sure you know that's what you are doing instead of simply being lazy as you wander around looking for where you want it all to go.

Yes, there are stories that come to you all at once, but my own example is of the kind that you start, run for a page or two, and stop, perhaps never to finish. It is the kind of story beginners are most apt to begin. They don't know how to get to the middle, the drama. Even experienced, published writers are not immune to jotting down openings that may never amount to anything— and these should be jotted down, just in case they do take you somewhere, sometimes years later.

So how to find a middle that is not *ad hoc* and false?

You have to ask yourself questions. How did the cat's teeth come to be capped? Was it painful to the cat? What kind of world is it in which you might cap a cat's teeth to hunt werewolves? Who are you, if this is a first person narrative? Is someone else telling the story? Is it true, or a tall tale? Who is the cat? Is the cat some sort of intelligent being, or just a cat?

With any luck I might be able to work this story out before I finish this essay. If I can find the middle, I'll know the end, and maybe even change the opening. Watch and see if I can do it, mostly by answering questions or finding questions I haven't yet asked.

How about: What do the man and cat have against werewolves? Answer that and launch into an action middle, maybe a hunt or two with outcomes.

36

With some kind of middle sketched, I can write a short summary of the story; then all that remains is to realize the outline, with all its setting, details, conflict, and resolution, but not too completely; you don't want to bore yourself to death; in writing, that would be as bad as knowing everything that's going to happen to you in your own future. Room must be left for inspiration, for sudden shifts, if any, the doing of what writers do—the finished sentence, the performance of the music written down in notes that make the story breathe.

Teaching is one thing; showing it being applied is another—and that's what I hope to show you actually happening in this essay.

Welcome to the middle of the essay!

The middle of my story must grow out of werewolf lore and what we can imagine to add to it, and from a bit of dentistry, necessarily, perhaps.

We've already introduced enough elements to incur some obligations. Yes, what you invent or assume *obligates* you.

Are there too many werewolves that have to be thinned out? Does our cat lose a silver cap and must have it replaced? Who is the dentist of our story? Is he still practicing? If not, the cat is in trouble.

A side thought breaks in on our planning of the story. Is this a fantasy, or does it only seem to be one, and in fact can be understood as science fiction? If we're clever enough we might have it one way or another, or both.

Now, how does a proper middle earn a story's end? Exactly how is this done? By providing enough of a conflict, enough of a problem, to demand a solution that is not easily guessed; it worries your characters into action, and must lead to a denouement—and to provide all this so that it seems right and logical (or illogical if that might make a satisfying end); you'll only know when someone else, even an editor, reads the story, or you will know when you've set it aside long enough to read it afresh. Mark Twain once said that a story must make sense; reality is under no such obligation, so don't confuse the two by appealing to reality, which sometimes does not make a good story but just runs on with no end in sight.

Back to our cat tale:

No one remembers when it all began, when we had to recruit our cats to fight the plague of werewolves. Many of us vaguely recall that long before that we hunted dragons and defeated them; and long before that we were all at war with each other and failed to defeat ourselves....

Is this a way into the middle of the story? You have to try it to know; it does have the virtue of being intriguing—but it just came to me, so I can't be certain; I may have to keep going to see how it might be a middle—if it can help me to generate an ending.

The passage suggests a predicament for our humankind, one that seems to have affected memory, hence our history.

Onward:

Maybe the cats know, but they don't speak; maybe they don't want to tell us, and have their own agenda. We often sit by a fire and I stare into my nameless cat's eyes, and she seems about to speak and tell me something....

Aha! Humans and cats may not be on the same page in this struggle against the werewolves. So what is the struggle? Will it ever end? This is getting complicated, and that's good, if you can work it. But it's part jam session with yourself and part thinking about what you want to do with your inspirations, those sudden invasions that come upon you and are so different from critical appraisals of what you've done.

Dorothea Brande, who wrote the best book about writing that I know about, *On Becoming a Writer*, and Frank O'Connor in *The Lonely Voice*, tell us that you should not be creative and critical at the same time. Write in heat but reflect in calm. This may be true of some writers and not of others; or it may be true of many writers at one time of day and not at night; you have to try it out and see. I'm trying to do both at the same time as I write this essay, but it is an essay, not a story, although a story is growing inside it at my insistence, which may be a good or bad thing. I won't know until it's all done whether it works, so Brande may have been right, in a complicated way, but will the story work outside the essay or only inside it as an example? I do not yet know, but we're in the middle of both story and essay, or so it seems, and must keep going.

One day, as we slept by the fire, my she-cat spoke to me. She told me that this was the safest way to tell about what had happened to my kind, where the wolves came from and why the silver capped teeth of cats came to be needed....

She said, "The wolves came from inside, materialized out of your deepest selves after a long history of warring amongst your kind, and you have no allies left to help you except your love of cats. The dogs went with the wolves, in a terrifying struggle amongst themselves, for the dogs were an old friend, whose violence against humankind had long ago been set aside, until the wolves brought it back. The wolves, as you may know, are also part of you, the vengeful part that now wars against us...."

What a mess!

But make it hard, even cruel, for the main character of a story, as Kurt Vonnegut has said. Show us what he's made of! Ask more questions.

> *"So why tell me this now," he asked. "Why tell me when I am asleep?"*
>
> *"Because I don't want to panic you," she said.*
>
> *"Panic me?"*
>
> *"Yes, the wolves are near to winning. All over the world we are telling this to you in your dreams, so you will awaken afraid but not in panic."*
>
> *"And then? What shall we do?"*

What to do, indeed? Is this hard enough, writer? Is there another question to ask, another—much harder—task to perform? We've stepped into it, deeply....

> *They woke up together, and saw that the wolves had surrounded their fire. It was red in their eyes at the edge of the clearing.*

Well, I told you that there are stories that don't come to you all at once, ending included. I wonder if O. Henry got to his next to the last paragraph before he discovered one of his famous endings. In my own "This Life and Later Ones" the last line came late, later than the ending itself, which ambushed me with its obligatory implication; I could not just put anything there. A writer can time travel, go back and fix the story to make sense after the fact; effective hindsight is the big secret of fiction, denied to us in real life. A story controls time, compressing events while struggling to maintain a taut line, as if all the moments were there while being skipped, as the writer decides, sometimes simply guesses, what he can leave out. The lesson in the understanding of this is that the middle must seem, for the reader, to be the longest stretch of time.

Still, don't give up on thinking up stories *all at once*, as exposition, development, and drama (drama is when the first two shut up), because that is one way to do it. Suggest it to your unconscious and see the brooms begin to carry endless buckets of water for you, as in "The Sorcerer's Apprentice." Keep a notebook handy, so you're not overwhelmed with trying to remember. Do not feel lazy about scribbling things down with a pencil. Get it down and save it—this is the great unseen middle of a writer's life, and may even be better than what you publish. You can always throw it away, ignore it, or have your heirs burn it.

And now back to our story.

What? I have no idea of where it goes from here. The wolves are waiting, like the electric bill. But one thing is certain. Endings are also waiting. More than one. Even a dozen.

To find an, even *the*, ending, you have to stay with the middle. Time out:

What kind of universe is it in which the best way to explain anything is with a story? To explain why people behave as they do requires a story; to explain why events happened in the way they did requires a story; a physics paper or a mathematical proof tells a story. It's a sequence, time's arrow, shot from past to future, carrying passengers.

What's the alternative: an eternal, changeless present, in which everything happens at once—or doesn't happen at all because it's all happened and is just sitting there.

Without a complex middle a story is static, uninvolving. That's why mediocre writers are so successful when they have a good story, however badly or well they tell it; they occupy the middle. A good chess player occupies and controls the middle of the board, and can strike out to the endgame. Life starts you nearly powerless; you struggle to control its middle; and then you make the best of the endgame; but it's the middle that brings satisfaction good enough to look back on in the denouement.

So what about our story? Can you do it, or is all just talk?

It needs more middle to point the way:

"You must kill them inside you," she said out loud, in a voice as beautiful as any meow, as powerful as any song that had ever soothed the savage beast.

Then:

He closed his eyes and reached inside himself to start the slaughter. Prides of silver-toothed cats readied to be let loose.

"I can't," he whispered into his abyss.

Red eyes blinked in the darkness.

Really? Is it that easy? That's it? He can't change?

You have failed?

Maybe, maybe not.

There's more to it than that; more middle will make this ending work just fine.

It does have something to say. You found that much.

It will do. Not great, but okay, when you think about it. Maybe better than that. Do more with details, and the prose; more middle will come to you, to develop the opening and delay the ending, which develops suspense.

Look at it again tomorrow, and maybe you'll tell yourself that's what you get for trying to grow a story inside of an essay.... Sometimes a story has to be simply okay.

It's been about middles, by way of beginnings and endings, because they are inseparable from middles. Einstein once said that past, present, and future are one and the same, that their separation is an illusion; maybe that's why beginnings, middles, and endings hold together so well in a well-knit story, and why you have to search out the ways they go together. Once they were together, but you tore them apart in writing a story....

But beyond these divisions of craftable time, illusory or not, there awaits the greatest middle of all: the work that will have to be done between the early and final drafts of a story. I imagined that this article might run some 5000 words to say what needs to be said, and maybe increase my pay. Beware, don't pad. Avoid the sagging middle made from ulterior motives (ask yourself what kind of writer you want to be, commercial or ambitious, although it may be easier to know your faults than to appreciate how good you are or might be. I pass this on because it seems that ideals should always be in the middle of everything we think or do). Long beginnings can bore. Middles can sag—but a great middle may enchant to the point where the reader does not want the story to end, and the very idea of an ending disappoints and confuses the reader; then a truly fine ending is needed to quiet the reader, to make him accept it without ruining the story.

The demands of the great middle work, coming between the first and last takes, may be characterized in the following way:

As a writer I have come to know what a story or novel, poem, play or screenplay should look like, how it should read, sound, and be, but it will always remain an open question whether I achieve it in a specific work, as I try, as I run the work to its finish, to success or failure.

To see, to feel, to understand what must be the realization of a work's ambition, its possibilities, in a reader's mind, summons the energy to make it so, and that may be the entire battle, or half, or even a quarter—as much as can be achieved before it can be judged a success or a failure; and that judgment may sometimes be the writer's to make, or for others to tell him, or for no one to know right away. A fine work of fiction is launched into the great middle of human efforts, with all that came before the writer's time pressing in on him and all that may still be looming ahead. Some say that a writer's best work comes at his beginning; some say in the middle; and it has, on occasion, come at the end of a career.

All of life is a great middle, not quite begun for any of us, and without an end. No story ever ends, but it must on the page.

All this can be said, and must be understood, and yet it is the smallest part of doing it, because there are some who, it is claimed, do it all without thinking and get it right.

And that's the end of my essay.

The only remaining hard part is THE TITLE, which some writers craft first and others last. Damon Knight once said that the title is the beginning of the story, and that he could not begin without a title. Most titles are not very good, because they require of a lot of effort, so most of them fill a space simply because something has to fill the space.

I'll leave this one at "Middles," but the real title is "The Importance of Middling Through." I rejected "Heft in the Middle."

JAY LAKE

ENDINGS

Jay Lake lives in Portland, Oregon, where he works on numerous writing and editing projects. His books for 2012 and 2013 include *Kalimpura* from Tor and *Love in the Time of Metal and Flesh* from Prime. His short fiction appears regularly in literary and genre markets worldwide. Jay is a winner of the John W. Campbell Award for Best New Writer, and a multiple nominee for the Hugo and World Fantasy Awards. He is represented by Jennifer Jackson of Donald Maas Literary Agency.

What Is an Ending?

The casual answer most readers and many writers would give to that deceptively simple question is that the ending is what happens when the story is over. But consider carefully what that means.

The prototypical ending that almost all children raised in the mainstream of American culture can recite is, "And they lived happily ever after." This classic plot summation flatly states all the hard stuff is over and life will proceed smoothly. The wolf has been slain, the wicked stepmother vanquished, the witch dashed with a bucket of water—the characters can all rest easy in the knowledge of a job well done.

Yet when in real life is this ever true? When are stories over? Something else always happens, even if it's only a funeral and wake. Prince Charming gets old, loses his hair, and has an affair with the stable boy. The Big Bad Wolf's six surviving littermates turn up and pillage Pigtown in vengeance for their slain brother. Chicken Little becomes soup with dumplings, and the plaster falls from the kitchen ceiling as steam rises from the pot.

The story is never over. It only comes to a resting place long and slow enough for the reader (and the writer) to take a deep breath and walk away without feeling unresolved.

Because in dramatic narratives, endings are resolutions. Not conclusions.

Hold on to that thought. We'll need it later.

What Is an Ending in Science Fiction or Fantasy?

Ultimately, the nature of the resolution presented in an ending arises from the writer's desire to sufficiently satisfy reader expectations. Most people read in preferred genres where they have familiarity with the tropes and conventions, and they can anticipate a certain kind of payoff. Classic category romance provides a very predictable boy-gets-girl (or perhaps girl-gets-boy) ending. In prototypical detective fiction, the sleuth solves the crime in some clever way, seeing that justice is done, order is restored, and so forth.

That's why people pick up these books in the first place. Comfort reading. Beach books. The accidental tourist, seeking familiarity.

The proper framing of this question is to ask what it is that science fiction or fantasy readers seek from an ending, and what makes those endings distinctive.

First, the idea of ending as resolution. Recall the classic seven-point plot outline:

- A character
- In a setting
- With a problem

- Tries to solve the problem
- Fails in some interesting fashion
- Tries repeatedly until they solve the problem either positively or negatively
- Validation is provided (at least to the reader)

Most narratives in the Western tradition follow this format. Your average bar story functions this way—"So I meet this gal on the road over there by Georgie's place, and I swear, she's carrying a squid and a cricket bat..." That opening promises something.

For the bar story to succeed, there must be a connection made between the squid, the cricket bat, and the woman carrying them. The strong implication is that this connection will be elucidated in some fashion that is funny, weird, or both. The weaker implication is that the narrator will be part of that process.

Likewise, the various genres of fiction. Detective stories present their main character in a setting where the problem—the crime to be solved—is the ostensible point of the story, in parallel to the progress and resolution of the narrative arc. Romance novels present their characters in a setting with a problem where the eventual outcome—the romantic connection—is the ostensible point of the story, again in parallel to the narrative arc.

And thus it is with science fiction and fantasy. Each genre has readers who come to the story with a set of expectations that match both the Western tradition, in the form of something much like the seven-point plot outline, and also with a set of expectations that matches their experience of the genre.

So what makes an ending in science fiction or fantasy? A resolution satisfies what it is that science fiction or fantasy readers in particular seek from that ending.

How the Two Genres Differ

In a fundamental sense, fantasy is a *normative* genre. By contrast, science fiction is a *non-normative* genre. This is, in turn, reflected in the sorts of endings that the two genres demand.

Normative refers to the idea that at the end of the story, when resolution has been attained, the order of the world is restored to the state it was in at the beginning of the story, ideally with improvements.

For example, mystery, in its prototypical form, is a normative genre. A crime occurs, the harmony of the community is disturbed, the detective investigates with eventual success, the guilty are punished, and order is restored to whatever degree is possible. The dead are not raised (that would be a different genre), but amends are made and lives go on. The whole point of such a plot is to validate the ideal state that pertained prior to the commission of the crime, and as much as possible to restore that state.

Romance likewise in its prototypical form is a normative genre. In this case, the state of affairs prior to the beginning of the story is not ideal, and the point of the story is to provide the needed choices and transitions to create that longed-for ideal state of the two love interests forming an appropriate union. Love is declared, the happy couple goes forth, and everyone's life is improved.

Consider the prototypical form of fantasy: epic or high fantasy set in a secondary world. A bucolic peace hangs over the land. Dark forces emerge from their ancient, brooding prisons of evil. Ambition and greed rampage widely. The hidden hero sets forth on the great quest that will vanquish the darkness, destroy the magic ring, and restore the true king to the Throne of Thorns. Great deeds are wrought amid despairing shadows, prices are paid, but ultimately the hidden hero triumphs and casts down the evil ascendant. Their bravery is revealed and is rewarded, and peace is restored.

At its heart, fantasy is about restoration of an idealized order that has been disrupted. That's a profoundly normative narrative. The point of reading fantasy written within this framework is the experience the glory of the journey through a different, beautiful place. (Much the same point as reading historicals, actually.) Some of the settings in George R. R. Martin's *A Song of Ice and Fire*, for example, are ridiculously improbable in any world bound by the laws of physics, but the Wall and the Aerie make for stirring reading and exciting locations for action within the story.

Science fiction in its prototypical form is about disruption rather than restoration. A change comes across the society of the story in the form of unexpected technological innovation, or perhaps the unheralded arrival of alien powers. The scientist-as-hero addresses the challenges caused by the change, but they do not do so by reversing them, or restoring the former order. They do so either through personal adaption, or through adapting the society around them. Great deeds are wrought in despairing times, prices are paid, but ultimately the scientist-as-hero triumphs and meets the challenge. Their wit and fortitude are rewarded, and the world is changed.

In other words, non-normative.

Reflect a moment on the reader expectations of normative fiction as contrasted with reader expectations of non-normative fiction. Those are two opposing approaches to the very meaning and intention of storytelling. It is ironic that the genres of fantasy and science fiction, each of which points in such different directions from their hearts, are conjoined twins within the world of publishing—written largely by the same pool of authors, represented by the same pool of agents, edited and published by the same houses.

Yet the two genres are far more different from each other than fantasy is from, say romance.

And in turn, this drives the narrative and dramatic requirements of the endings in each genre.

Distinct Demands of the Two Genres

Science fiction stories still require a dramatic payoff in the more usual sense—the story problem is solved (or not), the protagonist's goals are achieved (or not), the antagonist is thwarted (or not). However, at least in their prototypical form, science fiction stories also require a technological or scientific resolution to the story problem that was part of the original set-up. In other words, what is it that made the story science fictional in the first place?

This may seem self-evident, but consider a naturalistic narrative. For the most part, naturalistic fiction doesn't need to explain the world in which it occurs. Events, technologies, and processes within the story have a context generally shared by the author and reader. Science fiction by contrast embeds in its very fabric deviation from the naturalistic world in the form of innovation or differentiation. That's core to the reader experience of the genre, just as the relationship at the heart of the story is the key to reader experience of the romance genre.

A key part of that required technological or scientific resolution is the payoff in the form of a "sense of wonder," the term popularized by Damon Knight to describe the moment of expanded awareness of the universe and its possibilities that arises from the reading of science fiction. The reader expects to reach a point in the story where they say, "Oooh, cool!" This is not unlike the moment of satori that some literary critics speak of in naturalistic fiction, but in this context it is driven by the technological or scientific elements of the story rather than an unfolding of emotional or philosophical awareness.

While this sense-of-wonder moment isn't necessarily embedded in the ending of a science fiction story, it very often appears as part of the payoff, especially in short fiction. Novels create a different set of requirements, as the reader does not necessarily want to work their way through four hundred pages to reach that point. (We will discuss ending differences dictated by the various forms of fantasy and science fiction in just a moment.) Even when the sense-of-wonder trigger appears earlier in the piece, that frisson of realization should still form an integral part of the ending.

Fantasy stories have the same requirements for a dramatic ending as all other narratives, but they also have a fantastic arc that needs resolution. As noted earlier, science fiction's sense of wonder has a close equivalent in fantasy's secondary world experience—George R. R. Martin's elaborate castles—but that isn't critical to the conclusion of the fantastic arc. Rather, in prototypical fantasy the fantastic arc arises from the intersection of the moral and magical dimensions of the story. The ending in turn concerns itself with the resolution of that intersection, binding that with the narrative conclusion, just as a science fictional ending includes a reference to the underlying technological or scientific challenge of the story.

The key here is that in both genres, there is a second, relatively independent arc of the reader experience that parallels the primary narrative arc, and must be brought to an interesting and satisfying conclusion by the same storytelling process that wraps up the primary narrative arc. That genre arc meets different reader expectations in each of the two genres, but has much structural resonance between the two.

The Relationship between Form and Ending

Both science fiction and fantasy are generally viewed as having long-form and short-form expressions.

The long form is of course the novel, though granted that the formal definition of *novel* is any length over 40,000 words, that form covers an enormous amount of territory from the short, punchy works of the New Wave to the gigantic multivolume doorstops so beloved of high fantasy and space opera.

The short form is generally divided into short story (up to 7,500 words or so), novelette (up to 17,500 words or so) and novella (up to 40,000 words). Flash fiction (under 1,000 words) is often recognized as a category critically, though it gets little market support as a distinct format and almost no award recognition. Note that some genres do well in short forms—detective fiction, for example—while others are quite rare—romance, for example. In many respects, fantasy and science fiction share one of the most vibrant short fiction scenes of any of the major genres of fiction.

The ending requirements of each form are quite different. As mentioned earlier, the sense-of-wonder moment often is found at or immediately preceding the end of a science fiction short story, but those points tend to be far more front-loaded in science fiction novels, serving as plot drivers and pivotal character moments rather than as part of the resolution. Long-form fantasy endings diverge a bit less from short-form fantasy endings, as the moral resolution must appear at or near the end of the narrative of any length in order to justify and sustain the genre arc.

Novel endings are usually ramified and expansive, just like the books they serve. Novels are generally peopled with multiple point-of-view characters, and their primary narrative arcs are highly textured. Any idea sufficiently large enough to hold a reader's interest for several hundred pages generally requires this degree of complexity, and this degree of complexity, in turn, requires a sufficiently complex ending.

At the far end of the spectrum, flash fiction typically ends on a one- or two-sentence reveal with some twist or angle on the narrative to that point—much the same structure as a joke, in fact. Most flash fiction only holds one beat, one concept, one notion, so the payoff can be a counterpoint or expansion of that single story element.

The endings become a bit more textured as the short fiction categories expand. Short stories usually have a single plot arc and a small number of characters. They are still well contained, albeit with a bit more breathing room than their flash counterparts.

By the time we reach novelette length, the word count of the story permits the beginning of novel-sized complexity, much as implied by the name. Multiple point-of-view characters and multiple plot arcs emerge. This in turn begins to build up the requirements of the ending. Each of those characters and arcs must be dealt with, but even at this length, some economy of words is required.

Likewise, the novella is a form that grants further running room and breathing space for the author to work within. Stories at this length can in truth be "little novels," and lead to a similar complexity of ending as seen in the novel itself—expanded from the economy and punch of a short story ending, without reaching the fully expansive ending characteristic of a novel.

Idea Sizing, Promise and Payoff

Another way to approach the question of endings isn't from the perspective of the manuscript length, as discussed previously, but from the perspective of the idea size.

For the most part, manuscripts reflect idea sizing. If an author wants to write a piece about a low-grade industrial magician hitting bad traffic on his way to work, that's probably a short story, or perhaps a novelette. Frankly, that would fit into a flash fiction piece.

On the other hand, if an author wants to write a piece about a successful capitalist who has grown wealthy from manipulating the industrial magic talents of thousands of low-grade magicians, and is now fighting an equity takeover battle launched by the Old Ones Under the Hill, that's probably a novel.

So the piece about traffic might end on an ironic beat about homeless dragons on the bus bench, while the novel might conclude with a dramatic court scene featuring spell-based jury tampering and the attempted assassination of the Wizard-General of the United States.

But sometimes, an author may choose to take a different course. Imagine how dense and textured a short story about the magical capitalist would be. The idea would burst from the seams of the text. Even in four or five thousand words, such an idea would require a complex ending, far more involved than what a short story concept of more customary scale would need.

Likewise, if an author elected to tell a long, slow leisurely tale of morning traffic in a world of magical business challenges, that might be a novella or a novel with a slow, simple ending deriving its impact from the strong emotional thread at the center of the idea.

These examples also invoke the concept of promise and payoff. Stories create promises implied by a number of factors: genre, author branding, title, first line, first page, first action scene, initial characterization. The promise of the story is that the ending will be implicit in the beginning, but not obvious. In other words, the payoff.

These examples are linked to the idea size and manuscript length as well, as those in turn also create a reader expectation of the ending. The work of the author is to first understand those expectations, then meet them with the crafting of the ending.

Consider the low-level magician stuck in traffic. Genre is established: fantasy. Author branding is an external factor, important to the reader, but not part of the writing process. The title hasn't been specified yet, but let's call it "Number of the Bus." That offers both Biblical resonances and an accessible pun, implying either humor or irony. Assume for the sake of discussion that the prose on the first page sustains those elements.

Already we know more about how this story ends than we did a few pages ago. It's probably a clever twist that is more amusing than horrifying or saddening. There's likely to be a bit of erudition, some angle cribbed from Shakespeare, the Bible, or another classic source. The character begins to take shape from the assumptions—a younger woman of frustrated ambition and wry disposition, aware that she's being exploited but frustrated by her options, just as she is frustrated by the traffic problems in the story—and that in turn further influences the ending. What will someone like that choose to do, as opposed to the choices of a child or a retiree or a magical cop entering the situation?

Working the Craft of the Ending; or, How the Heck Do I Actually Do This?

The practical questions eventually intrude on any discussion of principle and theory. How does an author actually do the work of crafting an ending? For many newer writers, endings can be a critical challenge. For some established authors, they remain a struggle. Everyone has read published stories or novels that stop rather than end, for example.

The simple answer is that there is no simple answer. Like everything else in the craft of writing, endings require practice. Practice includes misfires and mistakes. But it also includes successes.

However, there are some basic guidelines you can follow taking into account much of what has been discussed here.

First, does your idea have a logical conclusion? Not simply a stopping place at which to end the prose, but a conclusion that points to some further action or development.

Second, is that ending supported by the genre in which you're writing? Meaning does the story action or character transition fit in with the reader expectations for the type of story you're writing?

Third, does that ending fit the length and form of piece you've written? If flash, does it have a single, punchy wrap-up? For a short story, does the narrative arc resolve with sufficient detail to provide resolution and validation? And so on through the various lengths. Likewise, does that ending match the idea sizing?

Fourth, does that ending deliver a payoff that meets the initial promise of the story? If you opened with a wizard on the bus, did you end with some act of magic, or magical restraint, that involved reaching his destination?

There is no checklist that will make sense on a widespread basis, but keeping these concepts in mind will help you sort out whether your ending functions. If it does not, either in your own eyes or according to critical feedback received, these concepts should help you troubleshoot the misdirected ending.

You have to follow the idea through to its unexpected but inevitable conclusion. Too simple and clear-cut, and it will not be satisfying. Too lateral to the beginning and tone of the story, and it will not be satisfying. There is no how-to on this, there is only mindful practice.

Which is, of course, true of so much in fiction.

The Value of Endings to a Developing Writer

As mentioned before, one thing many aspiring writers struggle with is endings. Ideas are the easy part. Framing them on the page and driving them to their logical conclusion is a lot more challenging. Giving them the wrap-up can be the hardest part of all. That's why you hear so many people talking about abandoning their novels or short story drafts because they thought it was going in the wrong direction and a better idea had occurred to them in the meantime.

If you don't practice endings, how will you ever get them right?

The value of endings to a developing writer is just that: practice.

The best advice in this context is also very simple. Finish everything you start. It doesn't matter if the story has utterly lost its way, and you write, "And then the sun went nova and they all died!" It doesn't matter if the ending you do write feels lame and unsupported. (That's what revision is for, after all.)

What matters is getting into the habit of writing the ending. Good, bad, or indifferent, get those words down on the page. That is the practice that will bring to you better understanding of the art and craft of endings. The temptation to abandon a project due to frustration, or the allure of a shinier idea somewhere else, can be very strong. All that will do is help you get better at beginnings, without ever writing endings.

One suggestion for a workshop is to take about ¾ of a finished story that's already in pretty good shape and pass it around the table. Each writer takes the partial home, writes their own ending, then comes back in the next session to review the different endings, why they worked and why they didn't. That should be an illuminating experience for everyone involved, especially the author of the first part of the work.

Stunt Writing and Oddball Endings

Sometimes there is a reason to end a story in a manner rather different from the resolution/validation model per the seven-point plot outline. Such variations can push the sensawunda button in a science fiction story, or cause the reader to reflect on the moral arc in a fantasy story. For my own part, I have deliberately written broken endings exactly twice in almost 300 published short stories. Still, it's an interesting technique to try in your work once or twice.

The clearest example I know of for this technique, and the place I learned it from, is the lyrics to Bill Morrissey's song, "Waiting for the Rain" on his album *You'll Never Get to Heaven*. The lyrics end about two lines before you expect, and so the listener has to supply the outcome of Chekhov's proverbial gun upon the mantel for themselves, according to their interpretation of the song.

Likewise, endings can occasionally be pushed to the beginning. Cordwainer Smith often employed this technique in his short fiction. Likewise some fairy tales begin so, providing you with the conclusion as part of the setup. "This is the tale of the scullery boy who became a king and how he came to win the crown...."

Such a technique emphasizes the journey of the story over the destination of the story, and so drives the reader down a different path. Like the broken ending, the end-at-the-beginning model requires active reader involvement and cooperation. And again, though hard to pull off, it's an interesting way to approach learning more about one's own endings.

A note about such stunt writing: I call these *parachute techniques*, because when they fail, they fail catastrophically. Many literary techniques can survive a fair amount of abuse and misuse, but this is not generally true of the broken ending or the end-at-the-beginning model.

In sum, if you write endings to every beginning you create, in time you will get better at endings. Be clear on what you think the reader expectations will be. Remember that endings are resolutions, not conclusions. Remember that endings need to fulfill the promise of the beginning. Remember that endings need to fulfill the genre arc of the story as well as the narrative arc. And don't be afraid to try something unusual once in a while, just to spread your wings.

Reading List and Examples

Very clear narrative and fantasy arc: Terry Pratchett's *Small Gods*; Jeffrey Ford's "Creation"

Very clear narrative and science fictional arc: Robert A. Heinlein's *The Moon Is a Harsh Mistress*; Ted Chiang's "Story of Your Life"

Broken ending: China Mieville's *Iron Council*; Jay Lake's "The Oxygen Man"

NAYAD A. MONROE
TIM POWERS TALKS ABOUT WRITING SPECULATIVE FICTION

Nayad Monroe writes speculative fiction, edits, draws digital illustrations, and reads slush for *Clarkesworld Magazine*. She likes to stay busy.

Tim Powers's first major novel was *The Drawing of the Dark* (1979), but the novel that earned him wide praise was *The Anubis Gates*, which won the Philip K. Dick Award and has since been published in many other languages. Powers has won the World Fantasy Award twice for his critically acclaimed novels *Last Call* and *Declare*. His 1988 novel *On Stranger Tides* was optioned for adaptation into the fourth *Pirates of the Caribbean* film.

Monroe: What makes speculative fiction interesting for you? Why do ghosts show up in your stories?

Powers: Well…. I started reading this sort of thing around age eleven. I remember in eighth grade reading H. P. Lovecraft, and it simply… It's as if my mind was a sheet of wet cement. Lovecraft imprinted it, and then it hardened. And even though I don't really read much science fiction or fantasy anymore, I can't think of a plot that isn't those things. If I tried to write a mainstream story about, you know, a handicapped child coming of age in Brooklyn, it wouldn't be chapter two before he started getting phone calls from his dead grandmother. Actually, it strikes me that here's the whole realm of emotions we can play with, in characters, what we can subject them to, and it goes from humor, love, anger.... One of them is supernatural awe, and it strikes me as arbitrary to say, "You're allowed to use all of them except that one." I think, that's crazy; I want to use that one, too! It's like giving an artist a whole palette full of paints, but you don't get blue.

Monroe: *So for you it's all about the supernatural awe?*

Powers: Certainly, and also I love grotesque, kind of Federico Fellini effects, the kind of insane parades and strange carnivals, and those are extra nice if there is a kind of supernatural element in them. So yeah, colorful grotesquerie, supernatural awe, supernatural horror... I suppose it's true that those are the ones I want to explore more than other emotions.

Monroe: *Are there any special challenges about writing science fiction and fantasy?*

Powers: Well, yeah, because a mainstream fiction writer just has to make the reader believe in *Miami*, or a TV set, but a writer of science fiction or fantasy has to present a world that at least in some core way is diametrically different from this one. And they have to put it in such a way that the reader vicariously experiences the difference, rather than just intellectually notes the difference. You have to not only know what the difference is, but you have to seduce the reader into coming along and continuing to think that your weird business is as real as the car they drove up in and the Marlboro cigarette they throw down on the pavement as they enter the building.

Monroe: What are you looking for when you read fiction? What kinds of stories appeal to you?

Powers: Actually, what I mostly read for entertainment, like if I'm getting on an airplane, is mysteries, suspense, thrillers. Dick Francis—I can read him infinitely. When I finish all his books, I can start over again at the beginning. Raymond Chandler, John le Carré, and then some mainstream people, like say, Kingsley Amis. When I do read science fiction or fantasy, it's usually re-reading, for one thing, and it's usually Heinlein, Leiber, Lovecraft, Philip K. Dick, Bradbury, kind of a fairly limited round.... Maybe because I love re-reading books. It's like going back to a city you remember fondly, you know, "Oh, I can't wait to see that street again." Except I'm thinking I can't wait to see that scene again. I do think it's important that a writer of science fiction and fantasy read very widely outside of science fiction and fantasy, because otherwise it's going to be like the hundredth photocopy of a photocopy. It's going to get very indistinct, and anemic, and inbred. It's beneficial to keep getting fresh tricks from the guys in the other areas. Like I'll be reading some Dick Francis, and I'll think, "What a cool trick. Oh, I'm going to try that. I want to do that in one of my books." Of course, it'll be a *dead* guy, instead of whatever Dick Francis had. A lot of perspectives and tricks and plot elements you can get from quote-mainstream-unquote, that transfer, that transplant, very nicely.

Monroe: In addition to reading in other genres, how do you feed your creativity?

Powers: I read a lot of poetry. I think poetry is real important, maybe for any fiction writer, but I think it's especially important for science fiction and fantasy, because with poetry, you're dealing with these images—because poetry really does consist of images more than words—which, if they're effective, they are effective because they ring Jungian silhouette recognitions in our heads. If you develop a taste for poetry you can see how, just like music, a line can give you goose bumps and a shiver. That's an awfully useful thing to know how to do if you want to write prose. Especially in our fields, because we do deal in the Jungian silhouette recognitions. Horror or fantasy very directly, but even science fiction—even the most hard science, strict physics, science fiction—is still, if it works, ringing those old Jungian, deep-water bells.

Monroe: Tell me more about Jungian silhouette recognition. What sorts of things are people recognizing, in a Jungian sense?

Powers: God knows. This is cheating, I suppose, but if you really could describe it you wouldn't need the symbol. There's something in a ring of standing stones, a cairn, a cross, a chalice, a sword, blood.... It would be difficult to say what things in our heads these ring, but they do ring something, and those are just objects, like sacramentals, but even certain stories do it. The story of the king who dies in the winter and comes back to life in the spring, who's connected: if he's healthy, the land's healthy, and if he's not, neither is the land. And God knows which is the "therefore," but they go together. In mythology, if you look at mythologies from lots of cultures, from Norwegian through Egyptian through Japanese, African, you'll notice recurrent characters. There's always a Fisher King, who's injured in some way that makes him sterile. And

who's fishing—even in the Arabian Nights there's a crippled king who's fishing, and I doubt the Arab writers heard the story from some primordial wandering Welshman. And there are lots of these characters that—Balder, Osiris—show up, and it would be naïve to think that the Egyptians heard about it from the Persians who heard about it from the Norwegians and the Japanese.... You've got to see that these come up spontaneously in the human psyche. God knows why, but since they do, it's fun to go by with a little hammer and tap on them.

Monroe: I guess it's important to be aware of those ideas, so you're not blindly reacting to them, but you're incorporating them.

Powers: Yeah.... I remember one book I was writing, in which a character was going across the Alps, and he's very important—King Arthur is what he is, reincarnated, although he doesn't know it—and I thought of this T.S. Eliot poem, "The Journey of the Magi," in which the Three Kings come to a low valley, but it's not their goal, and they can hear a mill wheel grinding in the darkness, and there's vine-leaves over the lintel of this tavern, and there's hands throwing dice, and a white horse runs by, and you just get the impression, "Whoa, oh my God, something big's happening here! What, I don't know, but it was big!" So what I did is I just took all those events out of the Eliot poem and put them in the book. I mean, I didn't use the wording, but I had the sound of the mill wheel at night, and so forth—I just thought, there's apparently some sort of heavy mythological baggage attached to these images. I'll put them over here, in my story. "What do they mean, Powers?" I don't know. But I hope they work as well in my book as they did in Eliot's poem.

Monroe: What got you started on writing secret histories?

Powers: K.W. Jeter and Ray Nelson and I had agreed to write a series of historical novels about King Arthur being reincarnated in various centuries, and so I wound up doing research and setting stories in historical periods, and I noticed how fun it was to get your world ready-made. Language, economy, cuisine, dress, weaponry—everything's already made! Maps! But it also seems to me that if you're writing a supernatural story, you're saying, "magic is happening in the world." Unless you're saying it only lately began to happen, then you're saying it's been going on for a while. And if you're saying it's been going on for a while, you have to explain how come people haven't noticed it going on all this while. Well, it's been secret. Only a few people knew about it. They've been trying to hide it. They didn't want you to know about it. So, almost by definition, a supernatural story set in the real world is going to involve secret history.

Monroe: I'm curious about things that work for you in your writing. I know that you draw a lot. Do you feel like drawing helps your writing at all?

Powers: In a very simple, mechanical way, in that I like to draw the floor plan of a room that a scene's happening in. And obviously this doesn't have to be artistic; it doesn't have to be straight lines and right angles. I just want a sort of blobby picture: here are the windows, here's the couch, here's the door, there's the refrigerator. Because I can look at that and remember that the refrigerator is over there by the window on the other side of the room, and not accidentally in a later scene have a character open the door and open the refrigerator a moment later. And I like to draw a scene from the point of view of a character, not, again, any kind of artistic thing, just blobs, just to say that "Oh, he wouldn't be able to see that building because the other building's in the way." Or, he couldn't see the door because of the car. Because the more accuracies like that you can provide, the more consistencies, it makes it a real car—more than if you didn't.

Monroe: When you're starting to write, on a given day, do you have any rituals that you do, any little things that help you get started?

Powers: Yeah... I always don't want to write. So I bring coffee in, and I turn on the computer. And then I leave the room. In fact, maybe that's when I make coffee, after I push the button. Then I come back, and the opening screen is on, and I'll double-click on AOL because I should check my mail before I do work. Ideally, mail and blogs will occupy me for an hour. But then I think, okay, you know what? You're supposed to be getting busy here, supposed to be getting a book done. And I think, *I don't want to.* And I look around to see if there are any old paperbacks I could pick up and read. And so then I'll open Microsoft Word. Then I'll leave the room. Then I'll come back and open the file, and leave the room. And then I'll come back and go to the end of the file where I'm actually at in writing, and then I'll begin to actually work. But I have to set up each step against huge reluctance. And then ideally I write a thousand words a day. Start by re-reading what you wrote the last couple of days, so that you come to the end running. Somebody pointed out that it's terrible to end a day's work at the end of a scene, because it's too final. You're going to have to be starting from zero tomorrow, so pursuing that, I like to end a day's work with an incomplete sentence. So I say, "After that, he..." On the theory that when I'm reading along tomorrow and get to that point, I'll sort of step off the edge of that sentence without even meaning to. "After that, he... woke up, he vomited, he shot at the fleeing figure," whatever. It's all to overcome my substantial reluctance to work.

Monroe: When you're talking about a thousand words a day, are you talking about seven days a week, or just weekdays, or... ?

Powers: If I can do five days a week of a thousand words a day, that's fine. Because something will always mess up two days a week. You don't have to plan it; God will provide it. In fact, really I suppose I'm lucky if I get five days a week. Yeah, seven would be nice, but kind of an impossibly ideal state.

Monroe: For an absolute beginner at writing science fiction and fantasy, how would you suggest that they should get started?

Powers: I'd say they have to read a whole lot, and in very widely differing categories. Read *Tom Sawyer*, read *Dr. No*, read *Treasure Island*, read a Robert Ludlum book. Because they need to be handy with the tools. They need to be able to see how they get used. Watching those writers is like a beginning carpenter watching some old guy working a lathe, or showing him how to drill some laminated material, or how to hang a door. So yeah, I'd say the first thing is to read a lot. And re-read stuff, because the first time you're just a dazzled passenger, but the second or third time you read a thing you're kind of looking over the railing and seeing how the engineering was done. After that, or at the same time as that, write. Write a lot. Finish what you write. Type it up, print it up in the correct format, and put it in the mail to an editor because, until strangers read a story you wrote, it doesn't really exist. In your drawer, or even among your friends, it's sort of an un-collapsed waveform. As soon as a stranger reads it, it collapses into either good or bad.

Monroe: What do you think of writing groups?

Powers: I don't approve of them. I mean, in college, I did go to this writing group where we would all have lots of pizza and beer, and people would read their poetry or stories, and that was fun, largely because of the pizza and beer. And it probably is good in that it encouraged us to have fresh work done by the next time the group met. But I think once you're publishing... I don't want to know what writers think of something I've written. I want to know what a couple of specific readers think of it, but I don't really have a use for knowing what writers think. I do think there's a tendency for people regularly attending a writing group to subconsciously, without deliberately deciding to, write to please those eight people. Those eight very idiosyncratic, distinct people. And being deflected from some direction because those eight people say they didn't like it, or even a majority of them didn't like it. It strikes me as too narrow. It strikes me that the sounding board a writer uses should be editors, not each other. The virtue of course would be that it does make you write. You're impelled to write something because by the next time they meet you want to have something to show them all. But it strikes me that guilt should really serve that function. I've never been inclined, since college, to join up in anything like that, because really, I find it much more useful to work from guilt and fear.

Monroe: But you have first readers, right?

Powers: I do have, ideally, two. My wife (Serena) and a friend, although the friend has now moved to Oklahoma, so it's really just my wife. And the reason I think my wife is a good first reader is because, a) she's intelligent and well-read, and b) she's not a writer. So when she tells me things that need doing, she's not saying, "The way I would have done it is X." If I showed it to a writer, that's exactly what I'd be getting.

Monroe: What techniques do you use to create problems for the characters in your stories?

Powers: Often I'll think, just to hold up as possibilities—and I'll toss them aside if they don't work—"What did he used to be very good at that he'd rather not do anymore?" Which is easily linked with, "Who did he used to be very close to, but he'd just as soon not see anymore?" Kid, spouse, parent, brother, best friend, what have you. Those often provoke some interesting problem. Also, I like to ask myself about each character a bunch of, ideally, random free-association questions like, "Did he have dogs when he was growing up? Did he ever live by the seashore? Does he like girls that are moody? Does he drink?" And then when I answer—I do this all at the keyboard, because you have to do your thinking all at the keyboard, not in your head—when I answer, I'll say, "Did he have dogs as pets when he was growing up? Yes." Then I'll ask myself, "Why?" And I'll say, "Well, his parents liked dogs, so there were always dogs around the house." And then I'll say, "No. Why *really*?" And it's when you ask yourself "Why *really*?" that you often come up with some interesting characteristics for the character. "Does he drink? No. Why not? He doesn't like to be drunk, doesn't like the taste. No. Why *really* doesn't he drink?" Very often you don't have to ask yourself too many of those questions, with those extensions, before you have some interesting characteristics and interesting room for problems to be fit into your characters.

Monroe: *What are some of the things to avoid when writing a story?*

Powers: There's something I think James Blish originally called the "idiot plot," which is a plot that only works because everyone in it is an idiot. They fail to think of the obvious solutions. That's a solid handicap. And I think, as a general rule, the thing that most makes a story not succeed is it hasn't been pictured enough. It's, like they say, talking heads in a white room. I'm always struck by how with real good pro writers, in every scene you could just draw the room. It's like you've been there now. Basically just not picturing it as really happening is a big flaw. Because with a lot of stories I read, I'll think, "You never expected me to believe that was real. You never believed it was real. It was sort of a stunt. It was a cardboard Godzilla. You didn't picture it as real."

Monroe: *Are there any pet peeves you have when you're reading a student's story? Anything you see a lot of that's just a mistake?*

Powers: Oh, you see too much of that default medieval landscape, the default medieval setting, where there's dark lords and princesses who are healers, and stuff like that. And I know Kathy Wentworth, who is first reader for the Writers of the Future Contest, says she gets way too many stories that begin with a character waking up, and it's especially bad if it's a character waking up with amnesia, in a featureless room, naked. This, of course, is probably caused by the writer having nothing much in mind, and thinking, "Well, have a guy wake up. What will he see? Well, I don't see anything. We'll have white walls, a blank room." So it's too obvious that you can see the writer walking onstage with a bucket of paint and a blank canvas. And any hint of sarcasm and tongue-in-cheek on the part of the narrator instantly turns me off.

Monroe: Most writers, when they're asked where their ideas come from, will either say "ideas are everywhere"—being very vague—or they'll give the standard snarky answer that they get them from a service in Schenectady. So I'm not going to ask you that. But once you have an idea, how do you figure out whether or not it's good, and what to do with it? How do you start to make it into a story?

Powers: Well, there will usually be some sort of fact or notion about how a couple of people could meet, or an interesting event that could puzzle someone, and, therefore, ideally the reader too. What I'll do is I'll talk to myself, and say, "What could this lead to, or what could it be the result of? What would have happened before that would have left this enigmatic thing happening to our protagonist? Give me something that would have led to this enigmatic thing that is likely to tumble the protagonist into an interesting adventure." And ideally, I think of three. It could turn out that he has a twin brother he never knew. Or it could turn out that he picked up the wrong box at the shoe store. Or he overslept and was ten minutes late tracing his route to work. And I'll extrapolate on all three, and once I've got a fair amount of extrapolation on three different ideas I'll say, "Which one do you like best?" I like to be able to consider several before deciding on one.

Monroe: What sort of questions should a writer ask while revising?

Powers: Where does the reader get bored? Often you can look at a scene and say, "All right, I've got a scene in a place with something happening. What else could be happening at the same time in this scene?" Serena once read a scene of mine in which two characters in a room at 10 Downing Street are talking and doing interesting info dump. One's telling things to the other which he needs to know. And Serena said, "That's one thing happening in the scene. There should be another thing happening in the scene." And so I had them still talking as before, but in addition I had—through pantomime and gestures—one of them indicate, "Install this microphone under the table." Which was much better. So I would say a writer should ask, "Should another thing be going on in this scene?" Not to take away any of the stuff that is going on, but to add another thing, too.

Monroe: You have a distinct way of writing. What are your thoughts on how a writer can develop her voice?

Powers: Somebody asked Hemingway once, "Where did you develop your style?" and he said it was an unwitting consequence of trying to make very clear the things in a scene he thought deserved extra clarity. You want to make certain things are very clearly in the reader's focus, in the reader's field of vision. It might be the emotional state of this person. It could be physical objects. Whatever it is, conveying it will impart a certain torque, a certain awkwardness, to what otherwise would be perfectly clear prose. And you kind of resist it, in that you don't want awkwardness, if you can help it. But in spite of trying to resist it, your concern that you really, really convey this here is going to torque it. And that torque is your style. So that really, ideally, if you were a perfect writer you wouldn't have any style. But since you have to strain a bit to get things done the way you want to get them done, that becomes your style. I do think the reason they vary is because everybody's got an idiosyncratic, different perspective, but I do think in every case it's a result of the writer's earnest and best efforts to make clear the things the writer thinks need to be made clear. Now, at first, when you first start writing, you're going to be writing imitations. All my early stories were imitation Lovecraft, Clark Ashton Smith, Robert E. Howard. But gradually you come up with your own perspectives, and then you're going to be doing your own style, but ideally, you will not be aware of it.

Monroe: Now I'm going to try to make you work. Suppose, for some reason, you were in a situation where you had to write a short story in twenty-four hours, and it's life or death. You really, really have to. Can you walk me through how you would go about starting, and developing it?

Powers: Yeah. I would tell myself—and all of it goes into the keyboard, you don't do it in your head. Every thought, even "um, um, um," goes into the keyboard.

Monroe: Why is that?

Powers: Because if you just consider a problem in your head, you will eventually come to a conclusion, which is likely to be stupid. And you don't remember how you got to it. But if you think into the keyboard and come to a conclusion, you realize your conclusion is stupid but you can page up, page up, page up and say, "*Here*, I was on to something. I should have gone this way. It was clever." So I would ask myself, "What has scared me? What has struck me as funny? What has struck me as tense and suspenseful?" It might be something in my actual life; it might be something in movies I've seen. And I might stop there. What did we have? Tense, funny, and scary. I would try to think of maybe three things in each category. And these presumably come with settings, and stuff surrounding them. And then I'd say, "Okay, what's the order of them? This comes before that one." And then I'd say, "Give me three characters to participate in this. I want to know how old they are, how tall they are, where they went to school, when they graduated, all that stuff, but mainly I want to know, for each one, what he or she would give anything in the world to get, and what he or she would give anything in the world to avoid facing. Then I would put them into that sort of bare bones story I've got, and I would try to find a position where they had to be in conflict. Where George could only get what he needs to get by denying Mary her chance to get what she needs to get. Or by forcing her to confront what she doesn't want to face. And I would remember that each of the one or two major characters has to be faced with a choice that can't be avoided, and has to be made, and lived with forever after, because I think a hard choice is always the hinge of any plot. And then theoretically out of that I would come up with a story.

Monroe: Would you try to come up with an ending—roughly, something to get to—first, or would you start from the beginning and develop it as you go?

Powers: Probably I'd start from the beginning, or even the whole thing at once, as if you're trying to move a bunch of pennies into some shape on a table. I might, in fact, think of a cool ending and try to think of the most effective way to lead up to it. But I would try to use provoking things—I'd ask myself that thing I mentioned earlier, "What is he real good at but is resolved not to do anymore?" He used to play piano world class, but now he doesn't want to do it. Because that has two cool things. It's promising that you're going to tell us why he doesn't want to do it anymore, and it's promising that he *will* do it again.

ORSON SCOTT CARD

ON RHETORIC AND STYLE

Orson Scott Card is an author, critic, public speaker, essayist, and columnist. His novel *Ender's Game* (1985) and its sequel *Speaker for the Dead* (1986) both won Hugo and Nebula Awards, making Card the only author to win both of American science fiction's top prizes in consecutive years.

I remember in my first conversation with a fellow grad student when I was (briefly) in the writing program at the University of North Carolina at Greensboro, this earnest young man said, "The first thing you have to do is develop a style. Until you have that, it doesn't matter what your story's about." This idea I found so appallingly ignorant that I wrote him off as a writer—only to find that he was one of the most highly regarded of the students in the workshop, and that his idea was widely held among literary writers.

Style cannot be taught, or even learned, not directly. Well, let me qualify that: A *good, distinctive* style that is a *pleasure to read* cannot be taught or learned directly. However, a stilted, awkward, affected, intrusive, and annoyingly artificial style can be taught and learned, and I daresay that such style is the primary achievement of most creative writing programs in American universities. I wish I had a dollar for every writing class that has begun with the statement from the teacher, "I don't know much about plot, so in this course we're going to concentrate on style."

What *is* style? It's often thought of as a combination of several things:

- word choice
- phrasing
- rhythm
- point of view
- evel of penetration
- attitude

The last three—viewpoint, level of penetration, and attitude—will vary from story to story. Furthermore, if the level of penetration is deep or if the story is told in first person, the word choice, phrasing, and rhythm should also depend on the character. But these aspects of style that vary with the particular story or character are more correctly referred to as voice, and this is at least partly the result of conscious development by the author. I can't get very far in writing any story until I'm comfortable with the narrative voice, even if I don't understand it. For instance, in *Hart's Hope* I found myself directly addressing the reader—a very old-fashioned style—until, about two-thirds of the way through the novel, I realized that this wasn't just the "dear reader" rhetoric of pre-modern novelists; the whole book was being written by one of the characters in order to persuade another of the characters to make a particular choice at the end of the story. I didn't have to change anything I had written before when I realized whose voice the story was written in. Without understanding why, I had been writing in that character's voice all along.

But this is hardly what anyone would call my "style." An author's style is usually conceived as something that can be found in all his works, certain quirks or mannerisms that constantly show up no matter what voice has been developed for a particular story. Scholars have done computer analysis of word frequency, for instance, and found that authors have quite distinctive and individual "fingerprints" of vocabulary that show up in all large-enough samples of their work.

Certainly, I have such quirks. For instance, I have a pronounced tendency to begin sentences and paragraphs with conjunctions. I didn't realize this, however, until it was pointed out to me by an editor, Andrew Offut, who regarded it as an annoying error. Indeed, it was annoying when done to excess—and to excess was definitely how I did it! Thus I have a tendency, whenever I notice myself doing it, to recast sentences so they stand alone rather than being linked by conjunctions to the sentence before. The result is, not the elimination of the "conjunctivitis," but a slight toning-down, so it's less annoying. Without thinking about it, without meaning to, I still continue to do it. Why?

Again, it took someone else to point out a plausible reason. Michael Collings, a poet and scholar who has written about my work, pointed out that the Book of Mormon, whose English translation is written in a style deliberately reminiscent of the King James version of the Bible, is extravagant in its use of precisely the same rhetorical device. This book, which I first read as a child and have re-read dozens of times since (and on which I have based many plays and novels), has inserted itself into my style, most especially when I'm recounting a story that feels important to me. That is, I unconsciously become "scriptural" when recounting pivotal events.

Having tracked down a possible explanation of one aspect

of my "style," let me point out the obvious: At no point in the development of this trait in my writing was I conscious of it, except to try to remove it or lessen its effects. It showed up in my writing because it is part of my innate use of language, arising from my early reading and my private hierarchy of levels of language formality and informality, intensity and casualness. I could not have planned such a stylistic quirk, and if I had, it would have been artificial and annoying—or, shall I say, *even more* annoying.

Every writer—no, every human being—has a distinctive voice, which emerges when we speak and, with luck, when we write. In certain kinds of writing—process writing, for instance, and legal writing, and highly formal discourse—such quirkiness needs to be held under control, or even completely submerged. That is the only value of such guides as *Elements of Style*, which is often touted as a writer's guide to "good style," but which in fact is utterly useless to writers of fiction; no, worse than useless, because it tears the soul out of phrase, sentence, and paragraph, leaving only a lifeless skeleton behind.

Fiction writing is the opposite of these. The living voice of the individual author needs to be heard; the reader is hungry for it, and delights in the music of it. However, a contradictory force is also at work: The reader wants to be guided through the story so as to be able to follow what happens and why without confusion or uncertainty. The author's rhetoric, therefore, must be employed in such a way as to achieve the latter purpose—clarity—without killing the individuality of his style.

Unfortunately, what happens in many, perhaps most, creative writing courses is that the students are encouraged—or encourage each other—to exaggerate or artificially simulate the individual voice quite at the expense of clarity, so that the reader is left perplexed, confused, unguided through the mapless landscape of the fictional universe. *All* that the reader is given is a voice, but one without content, as if someone were singing in your ear in a language you didn't understand. Very pretty, but after a while you start longing for some content.

Or maybe it's not so pretty. Because the "style" that intrudes is rarely the natural voice of a living person. Usually it's an affected, artificial style, chosen in imitation of other writers or invented in order to call attention to the writer at the expense of the story. Thus fiction, instead of being a storytelling medium, is transformed into a karaoke bar, where the entertainment consists of songs we've heard a thousand times, presented solely in order for singers to show off their imitations of other people's voices.

Is there nothing you can do, then, to enhance your own style, to improve it? Why, of course there is! But, paradoxically, you don't do it by working on your style.

In writing classes that I've taught over the years, I often get students who are victims of bad writing classes, whose "style" bears all the earmarks of too much effort to be "stylish." The result is invariably impenetrable prose; sentences that don't flow into paragraphs; awkward, confusing storytelling so you can barely tell what's happening or why. The temptation for the writing teacher is to say, "Your style is horrible! I can't make sense of this paragraph! Go back and do it over and make it read more smoothly!"

This, of course, is the *worst* thing you could say to such a writer. For the problem is that the writer is already thinking too much about the language he's writing. We've all had the experience of doing a physical process that is familiar to us—riding a bike or throwing a ball—and then, suddenly, we begin to analyze what we're doing, and in that moment we start doing it noticeably worse.

The intrusion of our conscious mind into the process makes us clumsy. We have to slow down; our reflexes were doing a much better job, more quickly.

So instead of telling these stylistically crippled students to concentrate *more* on their manner of writing, I force them to stop thinking about writing at all. In a trick I learned from Algis Budrys, I make them write, not stories, but *notes* about stories on three-by-five cards. "Don't write scenes, don't write the story," I tell them. "Just jot down what happens and why, as simply and clearly as possible. No dialogue! No description! Just what happens and why." Sometimes I have to repeat the assignment, especially the mantra "what happens and why," many times before the student finally stops trying to "write well" and instead merely writes it down.

Here's what happens: These problem writers, without exception, write better, clearer, *and more stylistically interesting* prose when they are not trying to write well. When their focus is on the story, and on helping the reader understand the plain tale, plainly told, their style improves dramatically and becomes far more interesting and individual than it ever was when they were trying to follow some teacher's or writer's instruction or (shudder!) example.

(So radical is the improvement that even *spelling* improves—for as often as not, serious spelling problems arise when students are thinking about spelling as they write. Think about it: Anyone who reads regularly has all the correct spellings stored somewhere in memory, and those correct spellings are more likely to emerge when you're not thinking about spelling than when you are. However, you're more likely to make homophone mistakes when you're not thinking about it—*their* for *there* is one of my common ones—so you still need to copy edit.)

Your natural style is already present in the language you use when you speak freely and fearlessly. That is the "style" you want to have show up in your work. Let other people figure out what it is—you aren't even thinking about it.

What *you* are thinking about is clarity—communicating clearly with the audience. But that communication must also include persuasion—you must persuade the reader to believe in your fictional characters and the world they move through, and also to care about what happens to people who, after all, don't even exist. The choice of language to achieve these ends is *rhetoric*, not style, and there is much to be learned about rhetoric. There are strategies and tactics, devices that work in some circumstances and not in others. If you must think about language, think about how better to achieve the goal of communicating clearly and persuasively with your readers.

This is the opposite, in some ways, of trying to create a "style." Instead of concentrating on yourself—how can I make people notice what a wonderfully stylish writer I am?—you are concentrating on the reader—how can I most effectively get the events of this story into the reader's living memory? The more you write (and the more other people read and respond to your writing, revealing to you the places where they become confused, bored, or skeptical while reading your tales), the better you'll get at controlling the rhetoric of your fiction. (And do yourself a favor—read Wayne C. Booth's, *The Rhetoric of Fiction*.)

Isaac Asimov, as a young writer, found himself imitating the admired style of his youth—a purple kind of prose that today would be execrable, but even then was no great thrill to read. Disgusted with the results in his own storytelling, he stopped trying to have a "style" at all, and instead concentrated on simple, declarative writing. In his own mind, he was removing all style from his work.

But I see it differently. Asimov was concentrating on perfecting his rhetoric, which he did better than any other writer of our time. His writing became so transparent, so rhetorically effective, that you are almost never conscious of the style, but rather are conscious of the ideas or events being presented. Asimov was criticized for not "characterizing" (though characterization is utterly unrelated to style), but what I find is that, on those rare occasions when the kind of story he was telling required deep character creation, he did an excellent job of it; however, the reader was never aware of it because the forward flow didn't stop in order to allow obvious, self-conscious character revelation.

In fact, Asimov became the foremost practitioner of the American plain style. Because he wrote science fiction, the chief gossips of the American literary neighborhood never gave him credit for his achievement, and in fact wrote disparagingly of his writing when they noticed it at all. But not one of them is capable of what Asimov achieved. And—most important to this discussion— his work had a definite, pronounced style, which is extraordinarily hard to imitate. His "fingerprint" is clear and uniquely his own. That it does not intrude on the reader's consciousness at any point during the process of reading is one of its virtues, not a failing.

Can you improve your style? Not directly. But if you work on your rhetoric—on communicating the plain tale clearly, credibly, persuasively—your natural style will emerge without any effort at all on your part. Other people will point it out; sometimes, when it is excessive, you will even want to tone it down (after the fact, though, *never* while you're writing your first draft). But you yourself will never give it a thought while writing.

Wait a minute—there is just one little thing that can improve your style, if you're up to it, if it matters to you. I'm a great believer in the music of language, the rhythm, the *meter* of it. Now and then, while writing, I become aware of writing with close attention to rhythm—usually a fluid iambic. This is usually second nature to me, because I spent so many hours and pages writing poetry and verse drama when I was younger. And in denouements, especially of my short stories, I sometimes write it as smoothly flowing verse, pure and simple, and then spread it out as regular prose on the page. Note the ending of my short story "The Fringe," for instance. But you'll notice that in so doing, I am not trying to make my writing "distinctive" or "stylish." Rather I am using iambic rhythm as a closure device—a rhetorical tactic—much the way that Shakespeare often closed scenes with rhymed couplets. A more formalized, structured language gives a sense of closure. Since this can be called "style," it's only fair to point out that I use it, and it is a deliberate, conscious language technique. But I must also point out that this is completely consistent with what I have said above: If I do it right, it is invisible to the reader, and it falls within the category of rhetoric—achieving practical effectiveness of writing—rather than style—causing readers to notice how "well" I'm writing.

PAMELA SARGENT

TALKING TOO MUCH, OR NOT ENOUGH: DIALOGUE IN SCIENCE FICTION AND FANTASY

Pamela Sargent is an author and editor. She has an MA in classical philosophy and has won a Nebula Award. She wrote a series concerning the terraforming of Venus that is sometimes compared to Kim Stanley Robinson's Mars trilogy, but predates it. She also edited various anthologies to celebrate the contributions of women in the history of science fiction. She is noted for writing alternate history stories. She also collaborated with George Zebrowski on numerous *Star Trek* novels.

"Nothing fills a page faster than dialogue," the writer said.
There it is, the blank page or screen, the intimidating and recurring challenge every writer must face. The temptation is to fill that page as quickly as possible, to advance the narrative however you can. Often the easiest way to do that, even for writers who are not masters of dialogue, is to get the characters talking. A few writers are even bold enough to begin novels or stories with a line of dialogue, something I don't recommend unless you possess the skills of the early Robert A Heinlein, who began his story "Blowups Happen" with the suspenseful line: "Put down that wrench!" Orson Scott Card also opened his popular novel *Ender's Game* with a piece

of dialogue that immediately rouses the reader's curiosity: "'I've watched through his eyes, I've listened through his ears, and I tell you he's the one." Writing good and convincing dialogue is usually enough of a challenge without relying on it to hook a reader right at the beginning of one's story.

Writing dialogue, whatever the difficulties, is generally easier than, for example, crafting descriptive passages, offering insights into a character's psychology, creating vigorous and absorbing action scenes, or presenting necessary exposition in a graceful way. Writers who harbor dreams of scriptwriting may be especially prone to fill pages with dialogue, but others also succumb, partly because dialogue is a shortcut and a very useful one. Sometimes a few well-chosen words of conversation can accomplish as much in a story as pages of description and exposition. There are also a fair number of readers who are more absorbed by stretches of repartee than by beautifully and poetically rendered descriptions. (Writers meet these people all the time; they're the ones who tell you they skip all the dull parts, often meaning those carefully wrought passages that cost you so much effort.) Better just to cut to the chase, or in this case, drop in on the conversation.

The strength of dialogue—namely that it can be a useful shortcut—is also its weakness. Writers who rely too much on dialogue risk leaving too much out. The writer may hear the characters clearly and easily envision the scene, but that doesn't mean that the reader will. (In a review of a novel some years back, Joanna Russ wrote that passages in that book seemed to be largely about names drinking cups of coffee, noticing the designs of ashtrays, or riffing on the furnishings in a room, the characters were so indistinguishable.) The beginning writer is likely to produce dialogue in which the reader will find it hard to tell one character from another. The useful shortcut can produce a story that is sketchy, in which too much has been left out.

"Listen up," the writer said.

Be a good listener. One way to learn how to write dialogue is to become a skilled eavesdropper. Listen to conversations in public places; pay attention to what people are saying and how they say it. You'll notice that most people talk in a casual way, using slang and some profanity. This does not mean that good dialogue should be exactly like actual speech, only that it should seem natural and convincing. Fictional dialogue that exactly mimics real life conversation would be close to unreadable, because most people also speak in incomplete and run-on sentences, sprinkle them with mannerisms ("you know," "it was, like, awesome," "know what I'm sayin'?" and the like), swerve from one subject to the next in the middle of a sentence, use extraneous words, repeat themselves, utter something completely irrelevant, and throw in a few "ums," "but, uhs," or "uhs" along the way.

In much daily conversation, people also tend not to listen very carefully, often because they are simply keeping track of what's being said while preparing their own response rather than actually paying attention. Keep this in mind if you intend to insert any exposition into dialogue. Drama can be increased if a character isn't actually absorbing crucial information being conveyed by a speaker. Having people talk at cross-purposes, or past each other, can further a plot or reveal character. Indirection can be used to heighten suspense, as can delay through dialogue. Space-filling dialogue can sometimes allow a story to "breathe." *Sometimes.*

The writer has to produce dialogue that seems like real speech without replicating it. Science fiction writer Robert J. Sawyer recommends recording an actual conversation and then transcribing it to see what actual speech looks like on a page. If that seems like too much trouble, I recommend getting hold of a raw unedited interview transcript; reading it, and then editing it into a readable interview. You should notice how much of the actual dialogue can be deleted and smoothed over while still retaining the flavor of the speaker and remaining true to what has been said.

You should also read as widely as possible, to see how other writers handle dialogue. Read the novels of Jane Austen and Ernest Hemingway while concentrating on what their characters say and how they say it. Read scripts or watch videos of plays and screenplays by such masters of dialogue as Quentin Tarantino, Harold Pinter, and David Mamet. Note how naturalistic their characters sound when talking, even though their lines are actually stripped-down, pointed, and distilled versions of how real people would sound. Pay attention to Hemingway's use of repetition and what it reveals about his characters, or Austen's use of irony. Which writers make you feel that you're overhearing a real conversation? Which writers catch you up in the conversation, and which ones seem unconvincing, and why? George Bernard Shaw can present characters thinking out loud, essay-style, and keep their talk gripping, but you have to be *Shaw* behind the words.

"I'd like you, Jonathan, to edit this interview," the writer said, "and Natalie, you can print out the transcript."
I always knew when my mother was either mad at me or had some serious matter to discuss, because she would utter my name for emphasis. "Pam, I have something to say to you." (When it was *"Pamela*, I have something to say," I knew that I was really in trouble.) I mention this because people don't normally sprinkle the names

of those they're talking to throughout their conversations. Think about it: when you're addressing somebody by name, it's usually because you need to get his attention, emphasize a point, or some urgency (or anger) is involved. (You might also do this if you're interviewing somebody on radio, and need to remind listeners of who is being interviewed.) People engaged in conversation know whom they're talking to, or who's talking to them, and don't need to remind one another of who they are. But beginning writers unsure of how to distinguish one character's way of talking from another's will often lard dialogue with proper names, in an effort to remind the reader of who is speaking and which characters are involved in the conversation.

I'll admit it: dropping proper names into lines of dialogue where they didn't really belong was one of my sins as a beginning writer. The writer who can fill in the scene, apart from the dialogue, and knows how to give each character lines that are recognizably that character's (sometimes this can be an idiom or expression peculiar to that character, or a speech pattern that other characters don't share) doesn't need to insert proper names to accomplish that task.

The student explained that he seemed unable to write dialogue that didn't sound stilted or forced. "Then I'll show you a few tricks," the writer said.
Every bit of dialogue presumably exchanged by the characters during the course of a story does not have to be on the page. Writers sometimes think they have to include much if not most of what their characters say to one another; this results in long, tedious talky stretches that don't really advance the story. Long passages of dialogue can be broken up by phrases that concisely convey what was said; Jerzy Kosinski's novel *The Painted Bird* is an excellent

example of a novel that delivers almost all of its dialogue indirectly through narration. If one character has to tell another something that the reader already knows, it's all right to summarize what was said in a line or two. Save the talk for dramatic scenes that require dialogue, ones where the dialogue is necessary to heighten conflict, reveal character, convey information, or create suspense. Ideally, you'll be trying to accomplish several of these ends at once.

"Here's the way to do it," the writer said /expostulated/ affirmed/ alleged/ declared/ replied/ remarked/ retorted/ mumbled/ murmured/ shouted/ shrieked/ whispered/ hollered.
Novice writers often worry that using "said" in all of their dialogue tags will seem repetitious or boring, and decide that the remedy is to use as many synonyms for "said" as seem appropriate. They mistakenly believe that doing so will make their dialogue stronger, or alert the reader to the way a character is speaking. Such substitutions are called "said-bookisms," and usually all they do is distract the reader from the dialogue and the story. A page full of substitutions for "said" is almost guaranteed to drive an editor crazy and convince her that she is dealing with an amateur.

"Said" is a very useful word precisely because it doesn't call attention to itself. Use any substitutes sparingly, for special emphasis.

"Now I'll pretend you're an idiot," the scientist said to his colleague, "and explain to you exactly how the alternative stochastic variability actuator and rotating transporter works."
In their efforts to avoid those long passages of exposition derided as expository lumps or data dumps, some science fiction writers will decide to include exposition in dialogue. There's nothing

necessarily wrong with that; people do lecture others while talking or explain things to one another. In fact, the first chapter of H.G. Wells's classic science fiction novel *The Time Machine* began with just such a conversation:

> "...You know of course that a mathematical line, a line of thickness *nil*, has no real existence. They taught you that? Neither has a mathematical plane. These things are mere abstractions."
>
> "That is all right," said the Psychologist.
>
> "Nor, having only length, breadth, and thickness, can a cube have a real existence."
>
> "There I object," said Filby. "Of course a solid body may exist. All real things—"
>
> "So most people think. But wait a moment. Can an *instantaneous* cube exist?"
>
> "Don't follow you," said Filby.
>
> "Can a cube that does not last for any time at all, have a real existence?"

The Time Traveller goes on to explain his theories to his friends at greater length, while they, who are ignorant of what he's been up to, respond with appropriate questions and comments at intervals.

Unfortunately, many novice writers of science fiction write scenes where characters discourse on scientific theories or on how certain kinds of technology work to characters who should already be familiar with those tools or concepts. Using dialogue to work in some exposition will only succeed if a character ignorant of what is being explained has a good reason for being involved in the conversation. (The beautiful-but-ignorant scientist's daughter used to serve this purpose, but I don't recommend using that particular kind of character these days.)

Know your characters well enough to be aware of what they should reasonably be expected to know, and avoid having other characters explain what should be well-known facts to them. Even if your central character is someone who has unexpectedly found himself in a completely unfamiliar place, as often happens in science fiction and fantasy, try not to write scene after scene of explanatory dialogue that will turn the whole story into a guided tour. Remember that good dialogue has to accomplish a number of ends besides explaining things to the reader. Good dialogue should, at a minimum, move the story forward, heighten drama, and characterize the speaker.

"Ruh-roh," the space jockey muttered, "my sprockets are so screwed."
Slang, for a writer, is like seasoning. A little can add flavor to the conversation; too much of it can overpower what is being said or what the dialogue is meant to reveal. For the science fiction writer, improperly used or carelessly written slang can completely destroy the suspension of disbelief required for the reader to enter the world of her story. If your far-future characters start talking about "chillin'" when they are relaxing, or expounding about how "totally awesome" a particular event is, the reader's going to have a hard time believing that he's in the twenty-eighth century unless the characters happen to be early twenty-first century time travelers. Too much slang can be as bad as extended passages of dialogue written in dialect—incomprehensible at times, distracting, exasperating, or unintentionally humorous.

Some science fiction writers try to get around this by creating their own futuristic slang, but to do this well, and at length, takes brilliance. Better to keep the dialogue as simple and clear as possible, with only an occasional invented word for a futuristic or alien device or concept, and make sure that any unfamiliar words are understandable in context. (Some novelists helpfully provide glossaries for their invented or unfamiliar terms, but having to flip back and forth to a glossary will distract most readers from the story.) Don't feel that science fictional dialogue is somehow different in kind from other kinds of dialogue—that it requires all manner of technical terms or weird language that sounds alien or futuristic but is actually meaningless. Science fiction movies and TV programs, with some exceptions, aren't necessarily the best guides to good dialogue, as many of them have characters who needlessly explain things to one another or utter meaningless lines full of pseudotechnical jargon, to name only two of a number of offenses.

Writers of fantasy, especially high fantasy, usually understand the wisdom of avoiding slang, unless they are deliberately aiming for humor or satire; they are likely to think instead that their characters should speak in highly formal or stylized fashion, or use a lot of highfalutin or archaic language. (I used to hear this kind of dialogue referred to as "high nasal.") Here again, it's better to keep things simple and clear.

A writer who offers a particularly good example of dialogue that seems natural is the historical novelist Cecelia Holland. Like science fiction and fantasy writers, authors of historical fiction are dealing with settings and cultures that are distant from their own; their characters must come across as people of their own time while remaining comprehensible to contemporary readers. Holland's characters are direct in their speech and use plain unadorned language; when they use profanity, they utter the same kinds of blasphemy and obscenity we often use, expressions that seem appropriate in context and serve the purpose of standing in for the actual words people in those historical periods might have used instead, words that would probably seem archaic, affected, or stilted rather than natural to contemporary readers.

Sometimes the use of invented words in dialogue will be necessary, but use them sparingly and only when essential.

"Change your mind?" the salesman asked.
"What have you got?" the customer replied.
In science fiction, and to some degree in fantasy, the use of familiar phrases of speech can often mean something completely unlike what the reader might normally associate with those phrases. As writer and critic Samuel R. Delany has pointed out, "The phrase 'her world exploded' in a naturalistic text will be a metaphor for a female character's emotional state; but in an sf text, if you had the same words—'her world exploded'—you'd have to maintain the possibility that they mean: A planet belonging to a woman blew up" (*Shorter Views: Queer Thoughts and the Politics of the Paraliterary*. Wesleyan University Press, 1999, p. 317). Another example offered by Delany is that of the clichéd phrase "She gave up her heart quite willingly." In Vonda N. McIntyre's novel *Superluminal*, this sentence refers to a character who has her own heart removed and replaced with a mechanical device.

Writing dialogue for a science fiction or fantasy story offers a place to transform such commonplace phrases; taking what seems to be a cliché and making it a literal statement is one way of impressing the reader with the strangeness and difference of your imagined world.

Consider the following bit of dialogue from Joanna Russ's short story "Nobody's Home," which takes place on a technologically advanced future Earth:

"Look," said Ann, and she pulled from the purse she wore at her waist a tiny fragment of cloth, stained rusty brown.

"What's that?"

"The second-best maker of hand-blown glass—oh, you know about it—well, this is his blood. When the best maker of hand-blown glass in the world had stabbed to the heart the second-best maker of hand-blown glass in the world, and cut his throat, too, some small children steeped handkerchiefs in his blood, and they're sending pieces all over the world."

"Good God!" cried Jannina.

"Don't worry, my dear," said lovely Ann, "it happens every decade or so. The children say they want to bring back cruelty, dirt, disease, glory, and hell. Then they forget about it. Every teacher knows that."

Immediately the reader is eavesdropping on a conversation between recognizably human beings who, whatever they might have in common with us, are both more advanced and perhaps more imperturbable than we are. Note what this piece of dialogue suggests and implies: a world lies behind those words.

"Open your ears to your voices," the writer said.
Paying attention to good examples of dialogue and picking up tips about writing dialogue can take a writer only so far. As writer and publisher Sol Stein once put it, "Dialogue is a foreign language, different from whatever language a writer has grown up using." In

other words, dialogue is not the transcription of spoken monologues or conversations, as I pointed out earlier, but something else entirely.

By accident, I was exposed to this foreign language in childhood, the best time to learn any unfamiliar tongue. My father, whose original ambition was to go into show business, owned several hardcover volumes of scripts by American playwrights; I was a voracious reader who would pick up just about any available book. As a result, my childhood reading included such plays as Moss Hart and George S. Kaufman's *The Man Who Came to Dinner*, Philip Barry's *The Philadelphia Story*, Elmer Rice's *Dream Girl*, William Saroyan's *The Time of Your Life*, and even Tennessee Williams's *The Glass Menagerie* and Eugene O'Neill's *Mourning Becomes Electra*, to name only a few. I didn't always understand certain words or references in the plays, but finding out what they meant took me to territory I might otherwise not have explored (although there are drawbacks to asking one's parents about exactly what it was that Kitty, the streetwalker in *The Time of Your Life*, did). I read these plays in an entirely naïve and unsophisticated way, envisioning the scenes in the same way I did scenes from *Bambi*, *Charlotte's Web*, Nancy Drew mysteries, and other childhood favorites. That what I was reading was almost entirely dialogue, with a few stage directions and only the barest description, didn't inhibit my enjoyment, and what I picked up unconsciously was just how much dialogue could do. Characters said things that they didn't really mean, or which meant something entirely the opposite of what was being said; they spoke lines that were deeply significant only in retrospect and revealed things about themselves that could provoke fear, suspense, laughter, or a shock of surprise, in me.

Later on, some years before I wrote anything for publication, I tried writing a story told entirely through dialogue. That story was a failure—I had left too much out—but another early story attempt taught me a lot even though that effort never saw publication. I was attempting something ambitious, a story told from several different points of view by prominent politicians of the day (Richard Nixon, Hubert Humphrey, Lyndon Johnson, and other such figures); not only did I have to enter their thought processes, I also had to give each of them some dialogue. That meant listening to their public pronouncements while also imagining what they might sound like in private conversation (since then, published transcripts of Richard Nixon's White House tapes during the Watergate scandal, tape recordings of Lyndon Johnson's phone calls, and other such documents have been of great help to attentive students of dialogue). I had to think about them as I would have any completely fictional character. I had to open my ears to their voices.

Ever since then, I have been unable to begin a story or novel unless and until I can hear a voice that belongs to that story. It might be the protagonist's voice, or the narrator's, but until I hear that voice speaking, and ruminating, and can start picking up on the voices of other characters, I'm not ready to write that particular story.

Think about people you know really well; can't you imagine what they might say, and how they would say it, in certain circumstances? Then consider the following: however well you know these real people, you can't read their thoughts, pick up on their hazily recalled memories and hidden secrets, or know them nearly as well as you will your fictional characters. (There will be times when your characters will seem even more "real" to you than people you actually know.) Knowing your characters in detail, and being able to tell when what you want to make them say isn't what they would say, or how they would say it—when a particular line isn't true to what they are and how you imagine them—is the key to writing convincing dialogue. The great goal of writing should be, as it is in the great trick of how the movie camera sees human faces, to read your characters' minds, without reading every word.

G. CAMERON FULLER

HOW ALIEN THE ALIEN: A PRIMER

G. Cameron Fuller's fiction and nonfiction has been published in newspapers and newsmagazines, literary and genre periodicals, fiction collections and classroom textbooks. As a writer, Fuller has won many awards in categories genre and literary, fiction and nonfiction, and he has been a contributor and columnist for *Writer's Digest*. As an editor, he has helped shape books that have won national and regional awards, both fiction and nonfiction. His crime thriller, *Full Bone Moon*, was published by Woodland Press, and he has begun to look for a home for a memoir, *On Balance: My First 25 Years with Multiple Sclerosis*. He currently writes and edits in Morgantown, West Virginia.

> "Art is a lie whose secret ingredient is truth."
> —Ian Leslie

Alien, Human, and Everything in Between

We begin with questions: Were the Na'vi, the cat-like blue people in *Avatar*, aliens? Was Hannibal Lector, a serial killer in *Silence of the Lambs*, an alien?

Many people would say the answers to those questions are, "Yes and no." But I would say, "No and yes." The Na'vi were physically alien, but they lived by values we recognize as human: love, loyalty, pride, harmony with the natural world. It takes more than blue skin and elongated limbs to make a character completely alien. In the ways that count, Hannibal Lector was truly alien, despite his physical humanity, his motives and actions unpredictable and unfathomable to most of us.

Often in science fiction, and in speculative fiction more generally, the "aliens" are recognizably human, sometimes more human than our neighbors. They are like the Na'vi, alien on the outside but very human on the inside. They are not much different than we are, not *other* or truly alien. They are *us*, in a funhouse mirror or wearing a rubber mask. But Hannibal Lector was just the opposite: A polite, aging psychiatrist on the outside, until his excessively violent actions made us see that something unrecognizable lurks inside him. Something alien.

The continuum between human aliens and alien humans can be used to assess any character in literature or the movies, but is especially useful for examining the aliens of speculative fiction (otherwordly figures of all sorts—sprites and Cylons, wookiees and werewolves and wizards, gigantic ants and gregarious rabbits):

- How alien can our aliens be?
- How alien *should* our aliens be?
- And why are they there in the first place?

True Lies

Science fiction has been called a *literature of ideas*, and often those ideas are played out in deep space among one or two or twenty alien species. Sometimes they sport horns, scales, or enormous heads, and communicate with squeaks and squeals and clicks. Some are lizards with high foreheads and some are single-celled organisms the size of blue whales. Their form is limited only by the author's imagination.

Or so it would seem at first glance.

In fact, the greatest constraint comes from the reader: Aliens must be *believable*. The reader of a book or viewer of a movie must believe that the aliens *could* exist, somewhere, at some time. Belief is fundamental to the success of any story, and that is as true of speculative fiction—stories set in places and times that are not here and now, and populated by characters who do not exist on the twenty-first century Earth—as it is true of any other fiction. Think of *Watership Down*, with its "talking" rabbits: fantastic as they were, the novel works because the reader *believes* in the reality of the story, at least while the book is open. Ultimately, a story must be *truthful*; that is to say, *true to life, true to the way life really is*, accurate in its representation of human experience.

All good fiction presents stories that the reader believes could actually happen. *It can be helpful to think of fiction as a really good lie.* And we all know that the most believable lies contain a great deal of truth. A successful lie must be believable at every point. Put another way, the less separation between truth and the lie, the more believable the lie.

The task of the would-be author of speculative fiction is to create characters and worlds that are not the here-and-now, but are close enough to it to be accepted by the reader as true in some fundamental way. One of the simplest ways to solidify your lie with truth is to make recognizable the underlying rules by which the characters and worlds function. The reader must be able to relate the story to his life, must be able to say, "Yes, that's the way things work. That's *real.*"

To return to *Watership Down*, the novel about sentient rabbits, for a moment. The setup is counterfactual, to be sure, but the situation is familiar. The rabbits are on a great journey, having left their warren after its destruction, and are wandering the countryside in search of a new home. The hardships, perils, and politics are all notably *familiar*, even though they are wrapped in an invented culture, one inhabited by rabbits. Except for the fact that the rabbits think and talk, everything from the physics to the plants and animals that inhabit their world is exactly like our own. In fact, humans exist in their world, too. The world of *Watership Down* is only separated by a couple of degrees from our own.

And that's key: The writer must be constantly aware of how far afield she can allow her imagination to roam before the alien—whether talking rabbit or sentient grasshopper—becomes unbelievable to the reader. Readers will allow a lot of leeway, but at some point it's just *too much*, too many degrees of separation from our experience to be believable. Few writers can pull this off, and it's a major accomplishment when someone can.

Characters must do things for understandable reasons, and the events in a story must be plausible; if something happens in the story that doesn't ring true to the reader's experience, the story will fail. Of course, there are levels of truthfulness and speculative fiction often pushes the boundaries of believability, but the story must fundamentally make sense. The aliens must be *real*, no matter how strange they seem.

That does not mean that the motivations for their behavior must be evident to the reader. Part of the thrill of writing and reading about alien characters is often that very mystery. Why did it do *that?* But the reader must believe that by the end of the story, the reasons will come clear. And the reason must be *true*.

Why Aliens?

Most of the aliens that appear in speculative fiction—short stories and novels, episodic TV and movies—are like the Na'vi. Or like Spock on *Star Trek*. Or even Chewbacca from *Star Wars*. Such human-aliens can be quite compelling, especially if used in a way that *comments on human relations or human society*. Alien characters are often used for precisely this reason. Star Trek is famous for this, from Spock to the Borg, the former a commentary on the hazards and benefits of emotion and the latter "about" the threatening nature of lock-step group behavior. Even though the format of Star Trek does not allow much nuance, social commentary is more compelling and less preachy when modeled by alien characters.

Aliens can also represent aspects of the world that we are wary of. In *Battlestar Galactica* (the new one *far* more than the original), the Cylons are alien representations of our fear of technology, a theme that Michael Crichton, author of *Jurassic Park*, explored in most of his books. In *2001: A Space Odyssey*, HAL was also a creation of humans and, like the Cylons, an alien representation of fear of technology. A list of examples of speculative fiction that grapple with the possibilities and perils of technology would be nearly endless.

Aliens in speculative fiction can also be stand-ins for real-world people or characteristics we dislike or fear. Writers of horror, in particular, mine this vein. Vampires, werewolves, zombies, all the classic tropes, explore our fears, as do more recent inventions that play upon our current fears: plague, terrorism, disconnectedness, powerlessness…. Choose a current fear to address and invent an alien and a plot with which to present it.

All these aliens, essentially twisted versions of humans or characters that exist primarily as commentaries on human individuals and society, may be fairly one-dimensional and relatively simple to create or they can be complex, vivid, nuanced. Either way, the writer must put the same kinds of thought into their creation. On one hand, the less alien the alien, the more human it is, the easier it is for some readers and viewers to suspend disbelief and go along with the story. On the other hand, the more *unlike* a human the alien is, the more *other than human*, the more compelling the character and the story is likely to be.

However you decide to portray your aliens, you should put them to this single test: *if your alien character could be replaced by a human character without significantly affecting the tale, you should probably just use a human character.*

The Birth of the Alien

When creating your alien landscapes—or the aliens themselves—you can begin by assuming that the standards of physics, chemistry, biology, and so on are as true for them as they are for us. The laws of nature underlie our experience and changing them more or less arbitrarily is almost guaranteed to result in an unbelievable story.

That does not mean, however, that life must necessarily be carbon-based or that the intelligent aliens must live on the land, but with a little research you can determine how, say, a silicon-based life form might develop or what kind of society might grow up if super-intelligent dolphins had opposable thumbs.

It also doesn't mean that you *can't* suspend *some* laws of physics or chemistry. For instance, in your world, maybe magic really works. In what are called second-world fantasies, stories set in an invented world, you have some leeway to play with natural law. Novels by Patrick Ross (*The Name of the Wind*, *The Wise Man's Fear*) are second-world fantasies in which magic is possible.

Remember, though, if you are writing about a world in which magic exists or mind-reading is possible, you need to be careful not to explain too much about *how* these things are possible. Don't overexplain. Readers are more willing to suspend disbelief in the unexplained than they are to accept an obviously absurd explanation. *Battlestar Galactica's* spaceships just "jump" from star system to star system; the authors were smart enough not to try to elaborate on the physics of *jumping*. The more explanation you provide, the more chance there is the reader/viewer will find a way to say, "That's not how things work."

For good sources of ideas for *plausible alien biology and behavior,* look to our own natural world. Networks such as Discover, Science, and National Geographic Wild are great sources for unusual information about the natural world. Books such as *Wicked Plants* and *Wicked Bugs,* by Amy Stewart, provide fodder for your writerly creations, and many other book sources are available and easy to find with Google searches or a check of the Amazon catalogue. The Web is full of sources weird and wonderful—videos, articles, books—and time spent on the Web will provide many, many ideas. Adapt unusual characteristics of Earth's abundant and diverse flora and fauna when creating your alien characters.

Whatever you do, you must make sure that every physical attribute of your aliens has a plausible reason for its existence. In other words, don't just willy nilly give your alien lobster claws, eyes on the calves of all five legs, or a mouth on the bottom of its left foot. Physical characteristics have reasonable explanations, and life tends to organize itself along certain general principles. Learn some of those principles (symmetry, form follows function, and so on) and use them.

If you want a planet on which life organizes itself along different general principles, fine. That could easily be the case on another planet. But don't simply create an alien, or a whole world of them, that appears to be haphazard and unreasonable. Unless you're writing an absurdist speculative fiction, like, say, Douglas Adams's *Hitchhiker's Guide to the Galaxy*, an alien that *has no reason to be the way it is* will considerably weaken your story.

The greater challenges, and greater pleasures to my mind, lie in the invention of alien culture. When done well, books that present entire alien cultures can be among the most engrossing examples of speculative fiction. *Left Hand of Darkness*, written by Ursula K. Le Guin (an interview with her, by Lucy A. Snyder, appears elsewhere in this volume), was among the first such books I ever read, and remains among the best. *Darkness* and the many books by Le Guin that take place before and after *Darkness* tell stories set within many of the worlds of humanity, each with its distinct culture, as do the *Dune* series, *Lord of the Rings* and its corollaries, and the many books of *A Song of Ice and Fire*. (It wasn't until years later that I learned an advantage Le Guin had when it came to inventing cultures: her father was Alfred Kroeber, the father of American anthropology.)

Alien cultures, when displayed in such depth, must be thought through completely. Everything in a culture influences everything else in surprising ways, and the major components of an alien culture must be outlined completely, even if the subtleties and details do not appear in the story itself. But religion, technology, language, economics, politics, art, history, the role of the individual in relation to the family, clan, and even society as a whole must all be considered. They all influence one another.

You probably need to do some research if you are not already familiar with how all these components interact. Excellent overviews of the way cultures work internally can be found in anthropological literature, and the more you know about how human cultures work, the more real your invented cultures will be. The more truth you know, the better your lie will be.

For instance: What is the nature of the religion(s) in your alien culture? What role does religion play? The society could be as relatively secular as that of, say, Germany, or as bound up with religious tenets as, say, Saudi Arabia. Or more extreme in either way. The role of religion in a society influences decisions large and small made by the citizens. Parents everywhere want what's best for their children, but while a German parent might believe the *best* includes an economically secure future, a Saudi parent might believe the most important *best* includes a future of subservience to the Will of Allah.

And it's the gradations and nuances of such social beliefs, both within the society and the individual, that make for a compelling, *true* lie. Cultural anthropology offers us this truism: *Behavior, no matter how bizarre it appears, always flows logically from beliefs about the world.* If economic security is essential, then robbing banks ultimately makes sense, even if unwise; if acting on behalf of Allah is most important, then any behavior the character believes Allah wants becomes logical and reasonable.

As you invent your aliens, their culture and their history, you should keep a small notebook in which to write down the details as they come to you. Some writers find this tedious and time consuming, but the more you work out before starting your story, especially if it is a novel, the more internal truth your lie will have. More backstory equals more truth, which equals a better lie.

Logical Unpredictability

Alienness, at its core, is about *unpredictability*. Alienness is about how far a character is from the reader's experience, perceptions, and beliefs. However, in fiction, *believable* aliens cannot be too far from the readers' world or the lie will not have enough truth to convince the reader.

Here is where the trickiest work comes in. To be alien, the character must be unpredictable, but not to the author. The author must understand the alien and its motivations, desires, and appetites, even when they are hidden from the reader. The less predictable the alien is to the reader, the more alien the alien will seem.

In its simplest form, the alien—like any character in fiction—should have desires and needs that it strives to fulfill. Recall the rule from anthropology: behavior flows logically from beliefs about the world. Aliens would have beliefs about the world that are *very* different from our own, and their actions, no matter how apparently bizarre or crazy, are perfectly in harmony with their beliefs. This is what makes Hannibal Lector's behavior so alien: his assessment of the world is completely different than our own. It's also what makes most aliens in speculative fiction seem to be merely humans with blue skin (or whatever). Alienness is about unpredictability, and the fewer assumptions about the world you share with the character, the less predictable, the less comprehensible, the more alien the character will be.

To be sure, motivations may change in different situations, just as they do with human characters. A generally peaceful person who is imprisoned and threatened with death might be willing to kill to escape; a serial killer on the hunt might choose to spare someone who reminds him of a valued friend from childhood. Be sure that your alien's motivations are layered and can vary according to the story's situation; doing this will add dimensions as well as unpredictability to your alien character.

Of course, the less you say about the aliens in your tale, the more alien they will seem to the reader. The alien is *most alien* when it first appears. The Na'vi, for instance, were the least humanlike—to both the human military characters and to the viewer—when they were first encountered. The more that was said about them, the more we saw their behavior and heard their words, the more like humans we learned that they were.

In the stories that reveal little about the aliens, they remain alien and mysterious and unpredictable. Such stories rely on readers' projections to make the aliens frightening or funny, fascinating or contemptible. The writer's task with such stories is to understand and anticipate the *readers'* reactions. Aliens who remain completely alien can be malicious or benevolent, but they ultimately remain *alien*.

Through Alien Eyes

Point of view is a tricky topic, and authorial choice about point of view is fraught with dangers. At its most basic, in English there are three choices: first person (*I did this and that*), second person (*You did the other*), and third person (*He/She/It did something else*). The first two have drawbacks: First person stories have an immediacy that is hard to match with either of the other two, and second person is difficult to sustain in a long work because the reader is naturally the *you*, and at some point is likely to say, "I *never* do the other thing" and close the book. Third person is by far the most common choice in fiction.

The other primary aspect of point of view might be characterized as *depth*. To what degree is the narrative inside the narrator's head? In first person, of course, the narrative is entirely in the narrator's head. The major drawback is that the writer can never say anything, add any fact or detail, that the narrator wouldn't know. Second person has largely the same limitations, although there is slightly more leeway in terms of an omniscient narrator adding little bits here and there.

Third person is where it gets tricky. The author can choose to be completely outside anyone's head, and the scenes and set pieces are described only by what the character did, what happened objectively. Or the author can choose to be inside the character's head to one degree or another. I group them with the general terms *light focus*, *medium focus*, and *deep focus* according to the degree to which the prose appears to be coming directly from the character.

These are the general opportunities and choices about point of view in fiction. (I highly recommend Orson Scott Card's book *Characters and Viewpoint*; Mr. Card spends an entire book explaining the mechanics, realities, and perils of choices about points of view.) But speculative fiction requires not only the typical point-of-view choices, but also must encompass the many creatures who might populate the landscape of the tale.

Perhaps the most difficult thing you can do in fiction is write from the point of view of an alien. When there are aliens in your story, it's relatively easy to portray them through the eyes of a human. You can use all the tricks—a fully imagined alien race or races and the inherent unpredictability of the intelligent other— and their alienness becomes part of the story and inspires respect, symbolizes human foibles, or incites fear according to the aims of your story. But to show the alien from the alien's point of view, that's an ultimate writing challenge.

One way is to return to the alien as not that alien, essentially a human with blue skin and extra long limbs. A Star Trek tale written exclusively from Spock's point of view would be a challenge, but not impossible. The more *alien* your point-of-view alien is, the more difficult it would be to write a convincing story.

You'd have to set aside the problem of writing in English and find a simple device to circumvent that limitation. Perhaps the story is discovered and translated by humans. Perhaps the alien is learning English, but has not mastered it.

They Are Among Us

In reality, we may have already encountered aliens without knowing it. I'm not talking about saucers and Grays and being probed in unmentionable places. It could be that a real alien would be so different from us as to be unrecognizable as an alien. Some unfamiliar object sitting in your doctor's office could be a sentient alien. It might be that the shadow you thought you saw on your porch while coming home the other night was a glimpse of an alien. That strange sound you heard in the yard or odd smell you caught on the sidewalk—nothing else, just a sound or a smell—might be an alien. Some of your dreams might actually be visitations. In other words, the alien could be so many degrees separated from us that we couldn't even apprehend it.

Of course, it would be difficult to turn an encounter with an alien that no one notices into a compelling story. It could be done—and has been—but most often involves the alien somehow becoming recognizable over time, the writer removing degrees of separation one by one as the picture becomes clear.

The writer's problem is to make aliens truly alien without making them so foreign as to be unrecognizable. For speculative fiction especially, your lie has to be separate from the truth, but not too far away.

NANCY KRESS

"THE GREEN-SKINNED ZORN LAUGHED WITH GRIEF" CHARACTER AND EMOTION IN SCIENCE FICTION AND FANTASY

Nancy Kress began writing in 1976 but has achieved her greatest notice since the publication of her Hugo and Nebula-winning 1991 novella "Beggars in Spain" which was later expanded into a novel with the same title. In addition to her novels, Kress has written numerous short stories and is a regular columnist for *Writer's Digest*. She is a regular at Clarion writing workshops and at The Writers Center in Bethesda, Maryland. She has also written several books on the subject of the writing craft.

There are two ways to pronounce "science fiction": with the stress on the first word or the second. I much prefer the second because it reminds us all that SF is, after all, storytelling and, like all stories, is about people. SF may (or may not) also be about science, but that's not the reason readers are perusing it. If they wanted pure science they would read *Astrophysical Journal* or *Cell*. No, SF readers are after stories that happen to characters. So are readers of fantasy, although without such a cute mnemonic reminder.

And characters—solid, interesting, plausible characters—feel emotions. Thus, you the writer will have to create emotions on the page. When we know what your characters feel—not just think, but *feel*—you gain several advantages:

- *increased reader involvement.* When something happens to us, we don't merely think about it rationally; we have emotional reactions to the event. When your characters react with anxiety, joy, grief, hope, disappointment, it's easier for readers to identify with and care about them. And if your characters aren't affected by what happens in the story, why should we be?

- *deeper characterization.* People are not all the same. When, for instance, aliens make contact with Earth, some people will immediately want to blow them out of the sky, some will want to welcome them warmly, some will search for ways to make money off them, some will have a religious conversion, some will hide in mountain caves. And some will feel two or more of these things simultaneously. We will understand your characters better if we know who feels fear, excitement, anger, envy, or relief ("Hey, we're not alone in the universe after all!")

- *advancement of the plot.* All of the above reactions to aliens lead to motivation, and it's motivation that drives plot. The protagonist who is suspicious of the aliens will, if he can, try to make sure they cannot threaten humans. This motivation—arising from feelings of suspicion—drives the climax of Larry

Niven's and Jerry Pournelle's *The Mote in God's Eye*. Even when a character is powerless to affect alien-human relations, her feelings about them may change her own life—this is the plot of my short story "Out of All Them Bright Stars."

Protagonists' Emotions

So you're going to make sure we get inside your protagonist's heart as well as his head. The first step is to be sure that you know what your character is feeling in the particular scene you're writing now. Writers do this in different ways. Some analyze what such a person might feel in such circumstances. Some go mystical, "becoming" the character in much the same way that an actor using Stanislavski Method tries to become the role she is playing. Most writers do both, consciously or not, creating a bond with the protagonist that tells the writer what the character is feeling.

Science fiction and fantasy protagonists, however, make more demands on the author than do characters in mainstream fiction. This is because your protagonist does not come from the same society as your readers. Consider: Elizabeth Bennet, in Jane Austen's *Pride and Prejudice*, is scandalized and shamed when her sister Lydia elopes. Twenty-first readers of romance novels find elopements romantic. Social mores change with time and place, and your character's emotions must seem natural in his setting, not ours.

A classic example of this is Harlan Ellison's story "A Boy and His Dog." Vic has grown up in a post-apocalyptic America where survival depends on scavenging and killing, in which he is aided by his sentient dog, Blood. Vic rescues a girl and they travel together for a while. But when Blood is injured and must have food, Vic feeds him the girl. This horrific story is about love, but Vic's experience of that emotion is shaped by the circumstances of his society: "A boy loves his dog." Similarly, both Paolo Bacigalupi's award-winning novel *The Windup Girl* (science fiction) and George R. R. Martin's wildly popular series *A Song of Ice and Fire* (fantasy) feature characters whose emotions of desperation drive them to brutality—and these are *sympathetic* characters. Their feelings grow naturally from their societies.

Not only violence rises from speculative societies. Ursula K. Le Guin's protagonist in *The Dispossessed*, Shevek, feels emotions much different from modern readers. He is disgusted by a street of nice shops, unhappy when a servant makes his bed, unwilling to accept an honorary doctorate from a prestigious university. All these emotions make sense in the context of the novel because Le Guin has so carefully shown us the world that shaped Shevek's feelings.

To bring this off successfully, you must first *have* a fully developed alternate society. This is one reason that speculative fiction is harder to write well than, say, the typical *New Yorker* story about marital angst in Connecticut. So make sure you fully understand the world you are creating. Setting spawns motivation, which both grows from and gives rise to emotion.

But—and here is where it gets complicated—only to a point. The stimuli for various human emotions may change radically from society to society, but the underlying drives do not. All humans experience fear, anger, love, desire for self-preservation. Both the causes and the expressions of these feelings differ, but the basic emotions are the same. If they were not, no literature would be comprehensible to readers.

Thus, your mission ("...should you choose to accept it...") is to create emotions in your characters that might arise naturally from a different society, but which are still feelings a reader can identify with. Another reason why SF and fantasy are harder to write well than is mainstream fiction.

A good example of this is Suzanne Collins's best-selling YA novel *The Hunger Games*. Collins's challenge here was to make a young killer, Katniss, both believable and sympathetic to readers. Had the book opened with Katniss killing another child, we would neither have understood nor accepted this action, and readers would not have identified with her. Instead, Katniss harms no one until Collins has made sure that we understand the complex society that has made it necessary for her to kill. It takes half the book to do this, as well as to show us Katniss performing acts of kindness and sacrifice that balance her later murders.

The Hunger Games embodies two important principles for portraying human emotions in an alternate society:

- Set the stage by putting the reasons for this emotion (and the acts arising from it) well in advance of the emotional scene itself. This means world-building with clarity and detail up front. Le Guin, for instance, portrays many aspects of the anarchic society on Anarres long before Shevek comes into opposition with it. By the time he does, we understand why because we understand this culture. The same is true of Katniss. What you *don't* want is to have to stop a scene in which a character is behaving against reader norms in order to explain why. We should already see why because we thoroughly see the differences from our world.

- The farther characters' emotions are from what we normally expect, the more explanatory background will be needed. Ellison's Vic, for instance, is a type not unknown in our world: an urban kid involved in gang wars, ruthless and sociopathic. Nor is he supposed to be likable. Thus, Ellison can sketch in his background, which is familiar to us from countless other post-apocalyptic scenarios. Katniss, on the other hand, comes from a very different social and economic structure, which Collins is careful to detail extensively so that we can not only believe but approve of her actions.

The second point is especially important if your SF or fantasy world is so different that the characters barely seem human any longer. Vonda McIntyre's brilliant story "Little Faces" features far-future mating rituals so bizarre that without much upfront scene-setting, we would not comprehend them, let alone vicariously share in them. And yet—a crucial point—these weird behaviors grow not just from a vastly altered human biology, but also from unaltered human needs: for connection, for love, for community.

So keep the underlying verities, but write their expression so as to match your fully explicated society.

Alien Emotions

What is true of human feelings is doubly true of aliens' emotions—whether the aliens are extraterrestrials, gnomes, angels, or vampires. If you want us to understand why they feel—and hence act—as they do, you need to give us the context. Otherwise, your aliens will end up seeming (1) arbitrary, which undercuts their believability, or (2) merely humans in funny suits, because we will impute human emotions to them as our default understanding.

Note: This does not necessarily mean long blocks of exposition. If the aliens are shown in their own society, we see the context as the story unfolds, which in turn will help us understand even really bizarre emotions. For example, James Tiptree's award-winning story "Love Is the Plan the Plan Is Death" has no human characters at all. Nor do Moggadeet, Lillili, and the other aliens behave even remotely as we do. But they do behave somewhat like Terran insects: emerging from cocoons in the spring, seeking mates that they bind with something like spider silk, being devoured by those same mates after impregnation. But these are thinking, feeling, insect-like entities who try to understand the accelerating climate changes on their planet. They also try, unsuccessfully, to resist their genetic instincts ("the Plan"). Their doomed efforts make them sympathetic to readers, as does their anguish at giving in to their more primitive impulses (and who among us has not done *that*?) But it is the planetary context and insect-analog that make them comprehensible—and without any exposition whatsoever.

When your aliens appear in our society rather than their own, you must find other ways to convey the cultural, social, and physical world that spawned them. Sometimes they explain their own background to humans, as do the vampires of Stephanie Meyers' *Twilight* books. Sometimes humans explain it to less knowledgeable humans; Frodo would not know very much about the Riders were it not for Gandalf's explanations.

You can also invert the process, especially if the aliens are not viewpoint characters. In this structure humans are initially baffled by the aliens, but then, after some contact, the humans infer the aliens' context from the emotions and behavior they exhibit. This works brilliantly in Ted Chiang's "The Story of Your Life," in which a linguist comes to understand the alien Heptapods as she studies their language. In fact, she not only understands them but is changed by contact with them, which supplies the emotion in the story.

However you do it, your aliens' emotions will be more interesting and accessible if we are given a context through which to interpret it.

Villains' Emotions

Villains are the neglected characters of speculative fiction. Not neglected in terms of action—they are constantly blowing things up, torturing people, putting spells on other characters, stealing and killing and plotting to take over the world. What is neglected is not their behavior but their emotions, which often come down to no more than "Die, you chump! Ha ha ha!"

There are SF novels with no real villains at all. The closest Le Guin comes in *The Dispossessed* are a pair of small-minded, morally obtuse characters, Sabul and Pae, living on two different worlds. No one could call either of them major brutes. Instead they sort of muddle through in their greasy-souled manners, one trying to share credit for the protagonist's scientific discoveries and the other spying, as he sees it, for the good of his country, which is about to go to war. They complicate life for the hero, but not as much as does mankind's large-scale and eternal problems of famine, war, and injustice, here not attributable to any one villain or group of villains.

What is notable, however, is that both Sabul and Pae have a clear motivation: envy. They are not acting from the notion of pure evil that seems to motivate so many fantasy and science fiction villains. Pure evil just doesn't work very well, because human beings, even the very worst of us, are not pure anything. We believe Sabul and

Pae because we can understand them. Who among us has not felt envy of another's superior accomplishments?

So give your villains emotions that we can understand and even identify with, even though we deplore the way they act on those emotions.

Complex Emotions

Just as your villain should not be pure evil, your hero should not be pure good. Not only is pure good not plausible, it is not even very interesting. This is a problem writers have struggled with as far back as Milton. In *Paradise Lost*, Satan comes across to readers as much more vivid and intriguing than does Christ.

The solution is to make your major characters a mix of traits: brave but envious, honorable but a little rigid, loving but easily cowed. Whatever blend of traits your character has will, of course, result in mixed emotions whenever he or she must act. This automatically raises both the interest and tension levels for readers, as they wonder which emotion will predominate and so dictate the next turn of the plot.

For instance, consider again sixteen-year-old Katniss from *The Hunger Games*. She has become responsible for feeding her family, which comprises herself, a little sister, and a widowed mother too depressed to function. Katniss feels multiple emotions about her mother: protectiveness, love, and anger that the woman will not assume the adult responsibilities forced onto her daughter. This mix makes Katniss a far more realistic character than if she were merely and consistently heroic.

Similarly, Frodo in Tolkien's *The Lord of the Rings* trilogy seldom feels just one emotion about his singular mission. In the beginning, he is torn between apprehension, reluctance, a sense of urgency, and even a certain relish for the adventure ahead. By the end, affected by the Ring, he feels a mix of possessiveness, anguish, desire to carry out his task, loyalty to his fellows and also a profound distrust of them.

What is true for humans can even be true of aliens, zombies, ghosts, or angels. Moggadeet, Tiptree's sentient and insect-like alien, nears autumn to find that his mother is ordering her sons away from her. She is in a terrible emotional frenzy. Instinct ("the Plan") compels her to eat any food she can find as winter draws near, including her own children. At the same time, her loving sentience wants to save them:

> "Go," she groans. "Go. Too late. Mother no more."
> "I don't want to leave you. Why must I go? Mother!" I wail, "Speak to me!" I keen my baby hum, <u>Deet! Deet!</u> <u>Tikki-takka! Deet</u>!

Eventually she drives him out just before she would have torn him to pieces, and then she hunts him the rest of the day, her anguish at having to do so much more compelling than a straight-forward bloodthirstiness.

Portraying Emotions

So once you know what your character is feeling, how do you get that emotion onto the page? The techniques for doing so are no different in SF and fantasy than in any other fiction. The least successful thing you can do is name the feeling: "Katniss was afraid." You want your readers to not just be informed of the emotion but to *feel* it. Ideally, the entire story has so involved readers that circumstances alone have induced the appropriate emotions.

However, several specific techniques can aid this process.

Show the bodily results of emotion. Here is Edward, in Greg Bear's classic SF story "Blood Music," looking at medical scans of his friend Vergil:

> The image took a second to integrate, then flowed into a pattern showing Vergil's skeleton. My jaw fell.
>
> Three seconds of that and it switched to his thoracic organs, then his musculature, and, finally, vascular system and skin.
>
> "How long since the accident?" I asked, trying to take the quiver out of my voice.
>
> "I haven't been in an accident," he said.

What Vergil has been in is far stranger than any accident. And what Edward is feeling—dismay, amazement—are conveyed better through his physical reactions than through naming those emotions.

Describe behavior prompted by emotions. Later in the same story Edward expresses his feelings about Vergil's situation through action, as well as through intentions for future action:

> I couldn't take any more. I made my exit with a few flimsy excuses, then sat in the lobby of the apartment building, trying to calm down. Somebody had to talk some sense into him. Who would he listen to? He had gone to Bernard....

Edward's shock and dismay are clear to us.

Give us the character's thoughts about the target of their emotion. Love is tricky to convey in fiction; all too often it shades into sentimentality and/or cliché. Ted Chiang avoids that in the award-winning "Story of Your Life" by giving us specific (and nicely ambivalent) thoughts that the protagonist has about the daughter who has been/will be born to her:

> It'll be when you first learn to walk that I get daily demonstrations of the asymmetry of our relationship. You'll be incessantly running off somewhere, and each time you walk into a door frame or scrape your knee, the pain feels like it's my own. It'll be like growing an errant limb, an extension of myself whose sensory nerves report pain just fine, but whose motor nerves don't convey my commands at all. It's so unfair: I'm going to give birth to an animated voodoo doll of myself. I didn't see this in the contract when I signed up. Was this part of the deal?
>
> And then there will be the times when I see you laughing.... It will be the most wonderful sound I could ever imagine, a sound that makes me feel like a fountain, or a wellspring.

The issue of time may be muddled here, but the love comes through warming as sunshine.

Let feeling be expressed directly, in dialogue. Del Pierce, the protagonist of Daryl Gregory's well-received 2008 fantasy *Pandemonium*, does not like a visitor at his mother's house:

> I stayed on the porch, getting colder in the breeze, as he finally climbed into the Buick. I watched him pull away and then shut the door behind me.
>
> "I don't like that guy," I said.

Lew laughed. "Pastor Paul? Come on, he's a nice old man." Mom shook her head, frowning. "What?" Lew said.

"How often does he come over?" I asked.

She shrugged and carried the coffee cups to the sink. "Once a month. Maybe every few weeks."

Lew laughed. "Hey, he got the hots for the Widow Pierce?"

Mom gave him the look that Lew and I called the Brush-Back Pitch.

I followed her. "What's he want? Do you *like* him visiting you?"

"Not particularly."

"Then why do you put up with him?"

No doubt here about Del's feelings of dislike and unease. They are made clear not only by his initial bald statement ("I don't like the guy") but also by his subsequent dialogue that refuses to let the subject drop.

Use figurative language to convey emotion. Sometimes similes and metaphors do a far better job with emotion than does straightforward narrative. When Jack Skillingstead's protagonist feels loneliness and an unexpected vulnerability in "Everyone Bleeds Through," an extended metaphor enables us to catch the feeling:

Rena was in the backseat of one of the cruisers. And I found myself in the unguarded fortress of my heart. Moat drained, portcullis raised, etc. Piranha flopped in the mud. A lonely wind blew through the open gate. That's what was left over.

What is your character feeling? Can you find a strong metaphor to embody it?

A Deeper Level

There are characters in fiction so real, so palpable, that they stay with us our whole lives. We *know* them. Part of that staying power is that we feel what they feel. Emotion may be expressed in understated prose, but the emotions themselves are always strongly felt by the characters. And, if you do your job right, by your readers as well.

HARRY TURTLEDOVE

ALTERNATE HISTORY: THE HOW-TO OF WHAT MIGHT HAVE BEEN

Harry Turtledove has been dubbed "The Master of Alternate History." Within that genre he is known both for creating original alternate history scenarios, such as survival of the Byzantine Empire or an alien invasion in the middle of the Second World War, and for giving a fresh and original treatment to themes previously dealt with by many others, such as the victory of the South in the American Civil War and of Nazi Germany in the Second World War. His novels have been credited with bringing alternate history into the mainstream.

It's mildly surprising that, these days, alternate history is mostly a subgenre of science fiction. Up through the first third of the twentieth century, it was the province—more accurately, the playground—of historians and politicians on a lark. As far as I know, it was invented by a historian on a lark, and not one notorious for larkishness, either. Writing around the time of Christ, the Roman scissors-and-paste specialist Livy wondered what might have happened had Alexander the Great not died in 323 BC, but turned west and loosed his Macedonians against the Roman Republic. Livy's opinion was that his long-dead ancestors would have handled Alexander's hoplite band just fine. My opinion is that Livy was a wild-eyed optimist, but that's neither here nor there. He wrote about not what had been but what might have been, and the die, as another Roman said, were cast.

More recent examples also have authors better known for things other than cranking out alternate history. In 1931, Winston Churchill published "If Lee Had Not Won the Battle of Gettysburg" in editor J.C. Squire's *If It Had Happened Otherwise: Lapses into Imaginative History*. Churchill wasn't in the British government at the time, but he had been, and, as some of you will recall, he would be again. Three years later, Arnold J. Toynbee, a historian of considerably greater acumen than Livy, wrote "The Forfeited Birthright of the Abortive Western Christian Civilization" as part of the second volume of *A Study of History*. This examines what a world where Celtic Christianity triumphed over the Roman variety and the Muslims succeeded in invading the Frankish Kingdom could have looked like. Both of these essays are party tricks, games intellectuals play.

So how did alternate history become part of sf, then? Well, for one thing, sf writers have written a devil of a lot of alternate history. Those in our field who've turned their hand to a-h include Murray Leinster, L. Sprague de Camp (whose "The Wheels of If" dramatizes the results of Toynbee's speculation), Poul Anderson, H. Beam Piper, Philip K. Dick, John Brunner, yours truly, S.M. Stirling, Kim Newman, William Sanders.... I could go on, but you get the idea.

And it's not surprising that this should be so, either. Alternate history uses the same extrapolative technique as other science fiction. It just plants the extrapolation at a different place on the timeline. Most sf changes something in the present or the nearer future and works out its consequences in the more distant future. A-h, by contrast, changes something in the more distant past and examines the effects of that change on the nearer past or the present. The tools are identical. Their placement, though, makes for different kinds of stories.

Outsiders still do pick up these tools every now and again. Over the past couple of generations, interesting alternate histories have come from writers as diverse as MacKinlay Kantor, Len Deighton, Robert Harris, and Philip Roth. In comments about *The Plot Against America*, Roth made it plain that he thought he was inventing something new and different with this whole what-might-have-been thing. He wasn't, but he produced an important book anyhow.

So you've decided you're going to write an alternate history this time around. How do you go about writing a good one, one that will entertain and interest your readers (without which, all else fails) and, with luck, make them think a bit, too? The first thing I need to warn you of is, it's not about Being Right. By the nature of things, you can't know if you're right. You are conducting a *Gedankenexperiment*, nothing more (and nothing less). You can reasonably hope to be plausible. Often—though not always—in this kind of story you will want to be plausible. We'll talk about how to manage that in a little bit. First, though, another word of warning.

Who and what you are will influence what you find interesting. This is not a hot headline; it is, in fact, inevitable. All fiction—not just a-h, not just sf, but all fiction—is not about the world you're creating. It's about the world you're living in. It's no accident that Livy speculated about an Alexandrian-Roman encounter. It's no accident that several nineteenth-century French novelists wondered what the world would have looked like had Napoleon won. It's no accident that Americans write so much a-h about their Civil War: it shaped who and what our country became. It's no accident that everybody seems to write a lot of alternate history about World War II; it's drowned out World War I in public perception of what made the rest of the twentieth century (and now the twenty-first) the way it is. Look at a different war and you look at a different world. A-h gives you a funhouse mirror in which to examine the real world and distort it in ways you can't do with any other kind of fiction.

Okay. Well and good. You can't help being who and what you are. History—real history—made you that way. Nevertheless, using your a-h story to bang a big drum for your political views has about as much chance of succeeding as using any other kind of story for the same purpose. People who already agree with you will go "Well, sure!" or, if they're old farts, "Right on!" People who don't will say less kindly things. Converting them ain't gonna happen. And selling your birthright for a pot of message (thank you, Ted Sturgeon) is almost always a bad idea. On second thought, delete "almost."

What should you do, then? The same thing you would do for any other kind of story: write the best piece you can. Even if you're writing something that seems to you far removed from your essential convictions, they will shine through anyhow. They can't help it. This is the famous realization that then-*Galaxy* editor H.L. Gold passed on to—once more—Theodore Sturgeon. He knew what he was talking about, too.

Let's look at some of the pieces that go into writing that best piece you can. A breakpoint for an alternate-history story needs to be both significant and interesting. The battle of Teutoberg Wald in 9 AD, which ensured that Germany would not become part of the Roman Empire, is one of the most significant in history. Europe looks profoundly different today because of what happened there then. If it had turned out otherwise ... well, who cares? Too long ago. It took me more than twenty years to come up with a story to follow on changing things there. The breakpoint also needs to be something that believably could have gone the other way. This is why writing a story where, for instance, the Native Americans fend off the Europeans is so hard: the conquistadors and their English and Dutch brethren simply had too big a head start on the people they found on this side of the Atlantic.

To figure out what you might change and to have an idea how you might change it and what would spring from that, you should be interested in real history and know something about it. You don't have to be professionally trained in history to write a-h, any more than you have to be an astronomer to write an sf piece involving one of Neptune's moons. If you are professionally trained, as I happen to be, that's an asset. But it's not a prerequisite. Still and all, you're unlikely to write a good story about Neptune's moons if you first have to hit Wikipedia to find out how many moons the planet has and how big they are. And you're unlikely to write an interesting a-h piece on early modern Europe if you have to look up the order of the Hundred Years' War, the Thirty Years' War, and the Seven Years' War. Doesn't mean you can't try something else. But that particular period might not be ideal for you.

When you look at what happens when you make your breakpoint go the other way, the way it didn't really go, you have to remember that you are *changing* things. You are changing them in all kinds of ways, and those changes will radiate out from your initial alteration. *Everything* will change, not just the stuff you're looking directly at. The farther from the breakpoint you go, the more different stuff will be. If Germany successfully gets incorporated into the Roman Empire, there's no way Constantine the Great gets born in an obscure provincial town more than two and a half centuries later. And double no way he fulfills a role in the changed world similar to the one he had in the real world.

This is one of those places where you can cheat. If you've got a world where the American Revolution never happened, Richard Nixon won't get born (one possible advantage to learning different words to the tune of "America the Beautiful"). But if you need a used-car salesman called Tricky Dick in the late twentieth century of that world, go ahead and stick him in. Just be aware that you *are* cheating, and then sin proudly. Don't drop him in there for no better reason than that you haven't thought through the consequences of your change.

Because if you are sloppy that way, people will spot it. There's always someone out there—usually, there are lots of someones out there—more knowledgeable about your topic than you are. In many ways, alternate history is still an intellectuals' parlor trick. Like any good fiction, it should evoke an emotional response. But it should also evoke one in the thinking part of the brain. And if your carelessness makes somebody crumple under the weight of disbelief that can no longer be suspended, you've lost that reader forever. You'll hear about it, too, in great detail. The Internet has made this easier and quicker, but it happened before, too.

A while ago, I said that you didn't have to be right when you were creating an alternate history: that by the nature of things you *couldn't* be right. It's still true. It has a back-asswards corollary, though. You'd better not be wrong about stuff you aren't changing deliberately. If you have British fighters accompanying British bombers on air raids over Germany in the early years of World War II, you *will* get letters—those alarmingly detailed letters— telling you those fighters couldn't have done that because they lacked the range. Again, someone will have failed to suspend disbelief and probably won't want to read on. Same thing goes for the shape of a '57 Chevy's tail fins and the price of shoes in 1902—or 1602.

If you aren't changing it on purpose and you can't be sure you're right about it, leave it out. A-h is a research-intensive subgenre; you need to resign yourself to that. If you can't, you'd once more be better off taking a swing at something else. This leads me to another point. The more of your research you do but don't show, the better off you are. "I've done my homework and you're gonna suffer for it" is one of alternate history's besetting sins. Expository lumps, friends, are right out. Research ought to be like an iceberg: ninety percent of it should stay under the surface of your story. If and when it crops out, it should do so in a few telling details, ones that make your reader feel *Well, of course he knows all that other stuff!* Tolkien, writing a fictitious history rather than an altered one, was particularly good at this.

One important difference between alternate history and other forms of sf and fantasy is that, with a-h, you aren't projecting onto a blank screen. If you're writing about the future or about a wholly created world, readers know only as much as you choose to tell them. The same goes for the people who inhabit your city on Tau Ceti II or in the imaginary Empire of Bebopdeluxe.

But what if you're writing about Chicago in 1881 in a world where the Confederacy won the Civil War? What if you're putting Abraham Lincoln in Chicago in that world in 1881? Everybody has ideas about Chicago. Everybody has ideas about what things were like for real in 1881. And everybody has ideas about Lincoln, too. In this altered world, what are some of the things you need to think about?

Chicago will probably be diminished economically to some

degree, because a Confederate victory puts a national frontier halfway down the Mississippi. But it will still be an important east-west hub, definitely a big city. Overall life in the new world's 1881 likely won't be much different from how it was in ours. Again, because of losing the war and being divided, the rump of the USA may well be poorer than it was in reality. If that's relevant to the story you're telling, you can find ways to indicate it.

But Abraham Lincoln, Lincoln in 1881, *there's* your challenge as a writer. In the real world, of course, he was dead, and a revered martyr north of the Mason-Dixon Line. Here, he'll be turning seventy. Is Mary Todd Lincoln still alive? If she is, what's she like? That will affect her husband. If she isn't, how and when did you have her die? (Isn't playing God fun?) That will also affect Lincoln.

He's not a martyr in the alternate world, obviously. Chances are he's not revered, either. After all, he's the President who led the USA into war against the CSA—and then lost it. Would he have won reelection in 1864, assuming the war was over by then? Chances are he wouldn't; you'll have to do more explaining if you say he did. What did defeat do to the Republicans? In real history, they dominated politics in the last third of the nineteenth century. Would they now? How do things look in Washington in the changed world (assuming you've left Washington in the USA)? What's Lincoln doing in Chicago, and how many people care?

And how does the brave new world he never really lived to see look to Lincoln? What does he think and feel about it? That's liable to be the crux of your story. He's watched laissez-faire capitalism take hold in the USA (and, don't forget, in the CSA) after the war. What does he think about it? He wrote some sharp things about the relationships between capital and slave labor. What would the relationships between capital and wage-slave labor look like to him? Has he ever heard of Karl Marx? What does he think about him, if he has?

I've offered answers to some of these questions in my novel, *How Few Remain*. The ones I proposed there certainly aren't the only ones possible. To me, alternate history is always more a game of questions than of answers, anyhow. The questions you come up with show what concerns you in the real world, even more than your answers will.

Real historians still play this game, too. Now they call it "counterfactuals." In my admittedly biased opinion, counterfactuals are much less interesting than alternate-history stories and novels. Why? Simple. Counterfactuals are illustrations of broad historical forces. Stories and novels are illustrations of character. People fascinate me; I have to confess that broad historical forces don't. You need both for any reasonably serious approach to the world's workings, but more people care more about people—a clumsy sentence, but true, and important to a writer.

Changing wars is an easy way to generate alternate histories. It's far from the only way. Altered history can spring from changed diseases. What would the world look like today if the Black Death had killed off ninety percent of Europe's population in the fourteenth century rather than "only" a third? What would it look like if HIV had spread out of Africa three hundred years before it really did?

You can play with geography, whether Earth's or the Solar System's. If the lump of rock in the next orbit out from the Sun had been big enough to hold a reasonable atmosphere, our Viking probe might have got a humongous surprise when it touched down there. Or—who knows?—their probe might have discovered us instead. If the Mediterranean Sea had never refilled after evaporating when the gap between Gibraltar and Africa closed up five million years ago, what might that part of the world look like now? If glaciations and migration patterns had worked out differently, the Americas might have been settled by *Homo erectus*, not *Homo sapiens*. How would Europeans have treated subhumans when they found them here? (This notion, and my book called *A Different Flesh*, spring from a speculation by the late Stephen Jay Gould. Inspired by exactly the same speculation, Roger MacBride Allen wrote the fine *Orphan of Creation* at about the same time. Each of us was fascinated to see how the other used very similar research materials—and we've been friends ever since, not least because of the coincidence.)

If gold hadn't been discovered on Cherokee lands in the late 1820s, the Trail of Tears might never have happened, treaties between the USA and Native American tribes might have been more respected, and things might not have turned out quite so bad for our original immigrants. Might—you can't be sure.

And if that fender-bender hadn't made you an hour late for your job interview, you wouldn't have drowned your sorrows at the place next door to that office ... and now, twenty years later, you wouldn't be married to your spouse. This is alternate history on what you might call the microhistorical level. Everyone has such stories. In a lifetime, you accumulate piles of them. It's so easy to imagine your life being different if you'd made another choice back then. And if it could happen to you, couldn't it happen to your country? Your world? Maybe Livy was pondering *his* long-ago fender-bender when he set pen to papyrus to talk about Alexander and the Romans.

I've mentioned researching a-h stories a few times. How do you go about that? If you want to capture the look and feel—and, most important, the language and attitudes—of a bygone time, use primary sources as much as you can. Primary sources are written by the people you're researching. A collection of Lincoln's speeches and writings is a primary source. A modern biography of him isn't—it's a secondary source. The advantage to using primary sources is that, with them, you are the only person standing between your source and your reader. Secondary sources add another layer of distancing, which isn't what you want. (Just in case you're wondering, it also isn't hard to find reprinted or plain used 1880s travel guides that will tell you more than you ever wanted to know about contemporary Chicago—what it was like before you went and changed it, at any rate.)

On this same principle, do as many things related to your novel yourself as you can, too. Nothing tells you more about what riding in an airship feels like than talking your way aboard the Goodyear blimp. You may not own an AK-47 yourself, but I wouldn't be surprised if you know someone who does. If you need to write about field-stripping one, watching where your friend has trouble will tell you where your characters may, too. If you set a novel in Hawaii, you should go there if you can possibly afford to; seeing the place at first hand will tell you more about weather and smells and such than you can get from a zillion books. (The same is no doubt true of Buffalo, but the temptations are fewer there.) And remember, for a working writer such travel is deductible. Save those receipts!

If you're working on something contentious, you will often find out that one side says one thing, the other side says something else, and if you didn't know better you'd be positive they were talking about two different incidents. How do you decide who's telling the truth and who's lying? How do you decide if anyone's telling the truth? You do it the same way you do when two of your children are squabbling over the last cookie: you weigh the available evidence, you make up your mind, and you take your best shot. Sometimes, when your kids are going at it hammer and tongs, you feel like smacking both of them, though I hope you don't. Sometimes you feel like smacking your sources, too. Most of the time, you can't, which is bound to be a good thing.

To sum up, you need to make up your mind about what your change is and what it means to things that follow upon it, and you probably need to do a not-too-obtrusive job of establishing it in the front end of your story. (You can do this too well. I had a story bounced by an editor who couldn't tell where the real history left off and the a-h began. I had, honest, made this Perfectly Clear—to me, anyhow. Not to him/her. The story eventually sold elsewhere, so I don't think the beam was entirely in my own eye.)

And, most important, you need to have your changes matter to the people in your piece, whether those people are real ones in new circumstances or figments of your imagination. If you don't do that, you may have yourself a cool counterfactual, but you won't have a story. People, what they do, what happens to them, and why, are what make stories. One reason alternate histories are hard to do well is that your need to do the background stuff can make you look away from the people in the foreground. Especially at the shorter lengths, you just don't have room to do that, so try not to.

The rewards are the flip side of the difficulties. A good alternate history can make your readers look at the ordinary, mundane world in a whole new way. The urgent desire to blow somebody's mind is a very Sixties thing, you say? Okay, I plead guilty to that. But in closing, I will note that a good friend of mine once said writing a-h was the most fun you could have with your clothes on. I don't know for sure that she was right, but I don't know for sure that she was wrong, either. Your next assignment, should you choose to accept it, is to find out for yourself.

JUDE-MARIE GREEN

LARRY NIVEN TALKS
ABOUT COLLABORATION

Jude-Marie Green lives in Los Angeles in close proximity to Larry Niven and other stars of the science fiction universe. She has published science fiction stories and articles on the Internet and in anthologies. She graduated from Clarion West in 2010. To learn more, visit her at judemariegreen.wikispaces.com.

Larry Niven is a science fiction writer based in Los Angeles, California. His novel, *Fallen Angels*, co-written with Jerry Pournelle and Michael Flynn, is a *Where's Waldo?* of local science fiction fandom. He published his first story in 1964: "The Coldest Place," in *Worlds of If.* He is justly famous for his Ringworld (Hugo Award for Best Novel in 1971) series of novels and stories and his Draco's Tavern stories always bring smiles to readers' faces. In addition to his solo work, he is well known for producing novels and short stories with other writers.

Jude-Marie Green: You're a collaborator! Do you know what we do with collaborators here?

Larry Niven: Pay them lots of money?

Green: *Only if they're good. And you're good, Mr. Niven.*

Niven: Call me Larry. I've collaborated in fiction with Brenda Cooper, Steven Barnes, and Jerry Pournelle, among others. They're good, too.

Green: *The Mote in God's Eye, Oath of Fealty, Lucifer's Hammer, and six others with Jerry Pournelle. Six with Steven Barnes. Two with Jerry Pournelle and Steven Barnes. One with Brenda Cooper. Three novels with Edward M. Lerner. And innumerable short stories and nonfiction articles. Written with others.*

However, I can get those details from Wikipedia. Or your own website, KNOWN SPACE: www.larryniven.net.

Niven: That's not my website. That's a fan-run website.

Green: *What I want to know, what the world wants to know, is why would you want to collaborate with another writer?*

Niven: To tell stories I can't tell alone. If I think the other writer can tell the story alone, I give it away. Sometimes the story was suggested to two of us. Once I wrote a story with Steven Barnes to teach him how to write in free fall (*The Descent of Anansi*). I write with Jerry [Pournelle] when there are too many characters for just me.

Green: *How do you decide to collaborate on a story? Do certain story ideas lend themselves to collaborative effort rather than single effort?*

Niven: Yes. Also, talking about a collaboration is recreation. It isn't work until you're writing text.

Green: I assume you have some ideas you'd prefer to develop yourself, something closer to your heart and theme as a writer, and some ideas that you think would work better with another writer's input. (I could be wrong.) How do you choose?

Niven: Anything personal, others stay out. I didn't let Ed Lerner into *Known Space* until I'd been going it alone for forty years.

Green: Edward M. Lerner is a hard science fiction author with degrees in physics and computer science. He collaborated with you on three novels: Fleet of Worlds, Juggler of Worlds, *and* Destroyer of Worlds.
How do you choose the different authors to collaborate with?

Niven: Carefully. Very carefully.

Green: In fact, didn't Jerry Pournelle choose you? He said if you wrote with him, he'd make you rich and famous. You replied that you were already rich, so Jerry said that he'd make you famous. Together, your collaborations have made your names and your stories well-known. One novel, Lucifer's Hammer, *was on* The New York Times *best seller list.*
I find it difficult to even discuss a story idea before it's written out. You have to come up with an idea and share it out with your chosen collaborator. What is your process?

Niven: Various. Jerry had a list of future possibilities that became *Oath of Fealty*. *Dante's Inferno* sat in my head until I invited Jerry in: he had the religious education. Robert Gleason suggested *Footfall* and *Lucifer's Hammer*. Sometimes I've sat down with someone and just talked until we had a story.

Green: Certainly you'd need to find another writer whose personality agrees with yours, or more importantly, whose writing is complementary, so that you don't constantly re-edit each other's efforts. What pitfalls of this kind of writing have you run into?

Niven: We always talk it out until we've got one story right to the end. Otherwise you can diverge.

Green: Success isn't guaranteed with any writing project. Do you have any collaborations or works that just didn't fly? Or maybe projects completed but didn't sell?

Niven: *Avogadro the Mole* is finished text still waiting for the third collaborator to do her illustrations. A computer game based on *Inferno* stalled at the beginning. Everything else has worked, even when we, Jerry and I, had to invite in a third collaborator. That's happened thrice.

Green: A writer's time being what it is, do you ever farm out your unfinished projects for others to complete?

Niven: I thought I'd given away a story to Jim Baen. He paid me a flat fee, but that was the principle: save me from having to write it. There was also a series based on *Armageddon 2429*, the original Buck Rogers story. Jerry and I wrote the outlines but no text. It stalled after a few volumes.

Green: What projects, collaborative and otherwise, do you plan for the future?

Niven: The fifth *Worlds* story with Ed Lerner. A novel that's fissioned into two, half written with Greg Benford: *The Bowl Of Heaven*. A near-present novel with Jerry Pournelle. I've got some ideas that would be solo flights, but they're slow off the mark.

Green: Do you have any general advice or words of wisdom for authors considering collaborating on a work?

Niven: Some can't do it at all. Don't try this early. Find your own craft first.

JOE HALDEMAN

HEMINGWAY TALKS ABOUT WRITING

Joe Haldeman is the author of 20 novels and five collections. *The Forever War* won the Nebula, Hugo, and Ditmar Awards for best science fiction novel in 1975. Other notable titles include *Camouflage, The Accidental Time Machine*, and *Marsbound*, as well as the short works "Graves," "Tricentennial," and "The Hemingway Hoax." He was honored as the Damon Knight Memorial Grand Master for 2010 by the Science Fiction and Fantasy Writers of America.

My first novel, *War Year*, came out to good reviews and no sales, as often happens. The most important review was a full page in *The New York Times Book Review*, which—along with many later ones—called my writing Hemingwayesque. I thought that was funny. My background was science, not literature, and the only Hemingway I'd read was "The Old Man and the Sea," in high school.

But it piqued my curiosity, and when my wife and I were on our first overseas trip, I picked up a Hemingway novel in a used-book bin in Marrakesh. It was *Fiesta*, the British title for *The Sun Also Rises*, and I was hooked. Over the next couple of years I read every Hemingway title, and then started in on the criticism and biography, which became a lifelong pursuit.

An early discovery, somewhere between my first novel and my second, was *By-Line Ernest Hemingway*, the collection of Hemingway's newspaper and magazine nonfiction.

Hemingway had made a deal with Arnold Gingrich, the editor of the new magazine *Esquire*, that he would write a monthly "letter," I think on whatever he wanted to write about, to help the magazine start up. They wanted Hemingway's name recognition, and he needed the money to help pay for his new fishing boat, the *Pilar*.

Most of the articles are amusing and informative, but one eight-page essay, titled "A High Seas Letter: Monologue to the Maestro," was more. It could change a person's life.

Before I started writing for a living, I read many books, probably dozens, about writing. I don't remember even one that was as useful as that eight-page article.

(To be fair, most books about writing aren't written by successful writers. It would be wonderful to find a book about writing by Hemingway or Fitzgerald or Shakespeare, but those guys are too busy doing it to write about how to do it.)

Hemingway did occasionally put observations about writing, usually at a metaphorical remove, into his nonfiction books, like *Death in the Afternoon* and *A Moveable Feast*. But I think the *Esquire* article is the longest sustained piece, and the only one that might be subtitled "How to Write Like Ernest Hemingway."

The context of the article is amusing. A young hobo, Arnold Samuelson, showed up on Hemingway's Key West doorstep, asking whether Hemingway could teach him how to write. Hemingway was amused, and wound up saying he would take Samuelson on as a deck hand when he went off to Cuba to fish for marlin, and would talk about writing if Samuelson would swab the deck and fix drinks and stay on the boat while it was moored. Samuelson played the violin, so Hemingway called him Maestro, often shortened to "Mice."

I want to examine the observations and assertions he made

to Mice then, in 1934, and see how they look now, from the point of view of a person who makes his living as a fiction writer, and occasional teacher.

That's a good place to start. One of the most famous quotes from that article is "If any son of a bitch could write he wouldn't have to teach writing in college."

Well, I don't "have to" teach, not for income, since I'm a reasonably successful science fiction writer. That technicality aside, I think his assertion was more true in 1934 than it is now. A writer can work for years on a novel and have it published to considerable critical success, and yet make nothing beyond a modest initial advance, five or ten thousand dollars (a 2004 survey gave the average first novel advance as $5920). My 1972 first-novel advance of $1500 would translate to $7500 today, and although I was glad to get it, it obviously wouldn't have kept me going for all that long.

So the writer has to do something to make money. He could follow Hemingway's example and go into journalism, or he could dig ditches, or he could teach writing. Doing that, he wouldn't have to deal with city editors or dirt under his fingernails.

In 1934, the newsstands were crammed with magazines that published nothing but fiction. They're not there anymore. The people who once bought them now watch Tivo-ed television or play with their Game Boys or computers. So it's almost impossible to make a living from short fiction, and pretty rare to make it from novels.

Mice asks Hemingway the kind of question a writer comes to always expect—nowadays it's "Do you use a computer? What kind?" He asked whether Hemingway used a typewriter or a pencil for his first drafts, and Hemingway answered, "Listen. When you start to write you get all the kick and the reader gets none. So you might as well use a typewriter because it is that much easier and you enjoy it that much more. After you learn to write your whole object is to convey everything, every sensation, sight, feeling, place, and emotion to the reader. To do this you have to work over what you write. If you write with a pencil you get three different sights at it to see if the reader is getting what you want him to. First when you read it over, then when it is typed you get another chance to improve it, and again in the proof. Writing it first in pencil gives you one-third more chance to improve it.... It also keeps it fluid longer so that you can better it easier."

That seems especially true nowadays. As a writing teacher, I sincerely wish my students would stay away from the keyboard until after they'd written a first draft. Most people under the age of forty can type with effortless speed. Their stories show it, coming out in bloggish careless sprawl. "They get all the kick, and the reader gets none."

When I first started to teach writing, there were no computers, and if I asked for a ten-page story, I'd get a seven-page story with three pages pasted onto the end. Now I get a seven-page story with three irrelevant pages stuck in the middle, thanks to the wonders of modern technology.

My own method of working is similar to Hemingway's. I write a slow initial draft by fountain pen into bound blank books, writing about 500 words on a good day, and type the text into the computer after each day's work, with some slight rewriting in the process. Of course when the novel's done, I print it out and give it a hard read—it's interesting, the errors that you can miss in a dozen readings on the screen. Then I get a third look when the copy-edited manuscript comes back, and a fourth in the galley proofs.

Mice asks him how much you should write in a day. He says, "The best way is always to stop when you're going good and when you know what will happen next. If you do that every day when you are writing you will never be stuck. That is the most valuable thing I can tell you so try to remember it."

It is really great advice, but I wonder whether Hemingway followed it regularly. In my own experience, I often stop *because* I'm stuck—or tired, or have come to the end of a section and want to think about it before going on.

Mice says "All right," and Hemingway continues: "Always stop when you are going good and don't think about it or worry about it until you start to write the next day. That way your subconscious will work on it all the time. But if you think about it consciously or worry about it you will kill it and your brain will be tired before you start. Once you are into the novel it is as cowardly to worry about whether you can go on the next day as to worry about having to go into inevitable action. You *have* to go on. So there is no sense to worry. You have to learn that to write a novel. The hard part about a novel is to finish it."

As to the actual daily amount, Hemingway did count every word and kept track of the totals. In a letter to his editor Maxwell Perkins, he said of publisher Charles Scribner, "Charlie's ridiculing of my daily word count was because he did not understand me or writing especially well nor know how happy one felt to have put down properly 422 words as you wanted them to be. And days of 1200 or 2700 were something that made you happier than you could believe." In those Key West days, Hemingway tried for 500 words a day, but said he could push it to a thousand if he wanted to take the next day off, fishing.

(As a footnote to this whole discussion, we have to appreciate the fact that few writers are reliable witnesses to their own work habits. It's not a profession that requires a time clock or overseers, and Hemingway, like most writers, tried different methods at different times in his life. When he was a young man honing his spare style, he worked in the cafés of Paris—his apartment was over a sawmill, so he didn't work there often—and by his own admission stacked up saucers, wine and brandy and beer, as well as coffee, while he was doing it. He later said that one should never drink before or during writing, but his wives and children and servants testified that he didn't always follow that advice. In Samuelson's recollection, Hemingway says, "A little is all right if you know how to drink, because it puts your mind on a different plane and it changes your ideas.")

When he was considering whether to take Samuelson aboard, Hemingway asked for a piece of his writing, and the boy reluctantly showed him a piece he'd done for a Minneapolis paper. "It was abominably written," Hemingway writes. "Still, I thought, many other people have written badly at the start and this boy is so extremely serious that he must have something: real seriousness in regard to writing being one of the two absolute necessities. The other, unfortunately, is talent."

You have to wonder how Samuelson felt when he saw that assessment in *Esquire* a year later. He did write a book about his summer with Hemingway, but never showed it to a publisher. His daughter found it in a collection of papers in 1981, after he'd died. She rewrote it—"whipped it into shape in much the same way my father was taught to whip big fish: by giving myself plenty of slack, striking some parts and pumping up others, reeling all the while, and finally mastering it." She proved to be an able collaborator with her father; the book is a fascinating record of a very odd relationship.

As a teacher I'm constantly faced with a seriousness-and-talent dichotomy. It's a rare class when I don't have at least one student who has the talent to be a professional writer; usually several do. Whether they're willing to suffer through the inevitable apprenticeship is another matter. Then there's also the sad inversion, a student who would kill to be a writer, but was born without talent. Some of them can make a living with words if they set their sights low enough and keep typing out repetitive formulaic yardgoods. But no amount of study or teaching will give them talent.

Amplifying on the difficulty of his sojourn with Mice, Hemingway says, "Your correspondent takes the practice of letters, as distinct from the writing of these monthly letters, very seriously; but he dislikes intensely talking about it with almost anyone alive.... If they can deter anyone from writing, he should be deterred; if they can be of use to anyone, your correspondent is pleased. If they bore you there are plenty of pictures in the magazine that you may turn to." (*Esquire* had just started running the controversial monthly Petty Girl erotic illustrations.)

Besides seriousness and talent, one of Samuelson's questions stimulated Hemingway to come up with another pair of qualities. He asks, "What about imagination?"

"It is the one thing besides honesty that a good writer must have," Hemingway says. "The more he learns from experience the more truly he can imagine. If he gets so he can imagine truly enough people will think the things he relates all really happened and that he is just reporting."

The next question sets up the heart of the article for me: "Where will it differ from reporting?" Mice asks.

"If it was reporting they would not remember it. When you describe something that has happened that day the timeliness makes people see it in their own imaginations. A month later that element of time is gone and your account would be flat and they would not see it in their minds nor remember it. But if you make it up instead of describe it, you can make it round and whole and solid and give it life. You create it, for good or bad. It is made; not described. It is just as true as the extent of your ability to make it and the knowledge you put into it."

The first question Mice asks is related to that: "What do you mean by good writing as opposed to bad writing?"

Hemingway says, "Good writing is true writing. If a man is making a story up it will be true in proportion to the amount of knowledge of life he has and how conscientious he is; so that when he makes something up it is as it would truly be. If he doesn't know how many people work in their minds and actions, his luck may save him for awhile, or he may write fantasy."

I have to wince when I read that, because my genre of science fiction *is* a subgenre of fantasy, technically, and if I didn't think it was possible to produce good writing under its aegis, I would write something else.

Of course, Hemingway wasn't talking about commercial or academic genres as they're pigeonholed today. Among the titles he said Mice had to read before he could write was *The Turn of the Screw*, arguably a fantasy story. I do think he was talking about pulp fiction. There's an expanded conversation in Samuelson's book, where he says that a book by Jack Woodford, *The Writing Racket*, said "a writer ought to start with the newspaper syndicates and the pulps." Hemingway's response was violent:

"That's absolutely wrong! Don't believe that crap. If you want to be a writer, make your money writing journalism or in any other way, but for chrissake don't depend on fiction for your living. If you start in writing phony stuff for the pulps, chances are you'll never learn how to write anything else. I've known a lot of pulp writers who thought they'd keep on until they'd saved enough money to live on and then write good stuff, but it never works. They find out they've never learned how to write. All they've been writing is shit and they've got so they can't write anything different."

Oddly enough, I give my students similar advice, though the pulp era is long gone. There is all manner of irredeemable sludge written under the rubric "sci-fi," and I tell them if they want to make a few bucks writing that, they don't need a college course. Just buy an armload of the books and read them as research, and then go forth and multiply. There are plenty of trees left to waste.

Hemingway goes on to say of his hypothetical ignorant fantasist, "If he continues to write about what he does not know about he will find himself faking. After he fakes a few times he cannot write honestly any more." I've seen that happen, but I'd assess it more charitably. Many people have the choice between two definitions of "serious" writer: admirable serious writing that pushes the critical envelope, versus serious writing as in "What is more serious than paying the mortgage and feeding my family?" Hemingway never had to worry about that. Before he was famous, he was wise enough to marry women who had money. One after the other, in fact.

To my mind, the least useful part of the article, in terms of advice, is when he talks about all the books a writer must read, a long and eccentric list. "Otherwise," Hemingway says, "he doesn't know what he has to beat."

Mice says, "What do you mean, 'has to beat'?"

"Listen. There is no use writing anything that has been written before unless you can beat it. What a writer in our time has to do is write what hasn't been written before or beat dead men at what they have done. The only way he can tell how he is going is to compete with dead men. Most live writers do not exist. Their fame is created by critics who always need a genius of the season, someone they understand completely and feel safe in praising, but when those fabricated geniuses are dead they will not exist. The only people for a serious writer to compete with are the dead that he knows are good."

This is a creepy foreshadowing of the disastrous 1950 Lillian Ross *New Yorker* interview, where he lurches drunkenly around New York indulging in literary pugilism: "I started out very quiet and I beat Mr. Turgenev. Then I trained hard and I beat Mr. de Maupassant. I've fought two draws with Mr. Stendhal, and I think I had the edge in the last one."

It's an odd locution, or conceit, since of course one writer can never really "beat" another. I'm sure Danielle Steel outsells Hemingway by a pretty large factor nowadays. Is that a technical knockout? I doubt that she ever bragged of having Hemingway on the ropes.

Those are just quibbles, though; macho radiations from American literature's premiere alpha male. But he was so much more than that. He studied what everybody else was doing, extracted what was useful to him, and took off on his own path. Sometimes it turned out to be a dead end. But until his decline, he could usually find his way back home. And a writer, like any artist, deserves to be judged by his writing, by the best of his writing, rather than whatever monument or ruin he makes of his life.

The last part of the article has this chilling exchange, mordant humor at the time:

> **Mice:** Do you think I will be a writer?
>
> **Y.C.:** (Your Correspondent): How the hell should I know?

Maybe you have no talent. Maybe you can't feel for other people. You've got some good stories if you can write them.

Mice: How can I tell?

Y.C.: Write. If you work at it five years and you find you're no good you can just as well shoot yourself then as now.

NISI SHAWL

UNBENDING GENDER

Nisi Shawl's *Filter House* won the 2008 Tiptree Award and was nominated for a 2009 World Fantasy Award. She's the coauthor of *Writing the Other*, a founding member of the Carl Brandon Society, and serves on Clarion West's Board of Directors. She was a Guest of Honor at WisCon 35 in May, 2011.

Why you're reading this article

Lots of speculative fiction is about sex. All of it is about gender, whether it wants to be or not. Because all of it will be read by people who identify with a gender, and read through the lens of that gender.

Gender is a highly sensitive topic, an individual experience with strong group input and community impact. Though there's lots of talk about gender bending, I find it more valuable to think in terms of unbending gender, of consciously ironing out the kinks one's peculiar perspective can put into gender issues.

This article discusses how you can write about gender consciously in the speculative fiction genre, with good intentions—and more to the point, with good results.

A word about these words

The word *gender* is often used nowadays to talk about people's sexual identities. Gender had an earlier incarnation as a linguistic term, and it's worth remembering that. In linguistic circles, gender refers to a way of grouping nouns together; different noun groups have different effects on the rest of any sentence in which they appear. English nouns have no gender. Nouns in other languages have from two to twenty genders. Two to *twenty*. Most language students are familiar with masculine and feminine as linguistic genders, and are used to changing adjectives and so on to reflect the gender of the nouns they go with. In French, books are masculine and windows are feminine.

Masculine, feminine; that's two. Some languages add a gender called *neuter*. So what about the other seventeen? Well, a gender label can refer to a group of nouns whose members are flammable. Or mobile. Or abstract. Gender, in linguistic terms, is not a binary: it's not on/off, yes/no, masculine/feminine. And it's not even confined to two dimensions, with masculine and feminine as extremes along a single axis and neuter in the middle.

Gender is all over the place, linguistically speaking. As creators of speculative fiction we need to keep that in mind. It makes a handy analogy when thinking and talking about how to represent gender as sexual identity. Which is also not a binary.

Mostly in this article I'll use the word *sex* to talk about something you do, and the word *sexuality* to describe one's feelings and attitudes about one's sexual activity. I'll use *gender* as a more inclusive word covering social roles, self-image, and other areas related to what a person's sexual identity means.*

Vive les differences

You want to write science fiction and fantasy, yes? Let's assume for the moment your stories concern human characters. You're a human. Makes it that much easier. All you have to do is look around you and base your work on what you see. Extrapolate from your surroundings. Except...

Except what you see is influenced by who you are. And where you are. Keeping your own perspective in mind can mean you'll alienate fewer readers whose demographics don't match yours. And it can prevent your fiction from coming to feel dated in the embarrassing way of much "Golden Age" SF. You know what I'm talking about: those stories steeped in the social, cultural, and economic values of twentieth century middle-class white USians despite ostensibly

---

*Here are some additional useful terms:

- Someone who is **transgendered** experiences a mismatch between their psychological gender and the physical one they were born with; generally speaking, transgender men were born as females and transgender women as males. Cosmetics, surgery, hormones, and clothing are among the ways transgender men and women bring their bodies' genders into alignment with those of their minds and emotions.
- Someone who is **cisgendered** doesn't experience this mismatch; their physical birth gender matches their psychological gender.
- **Heterosexuals** are sexually attracted to people of a different gender and/or sex.
- **Homosexuals** are sexually attracted to people of the same gender and/or sex. Tanith Lee used the phrases "mirror-biased" and "mb" to describe this idea in her novels *Don't Bite the Sun* and *Drinking Sapphire Wine*. Homosexual women are often referred to as "lesbians"; "gay" usually refers to a homosexual man, though not always.
- People formerly known as hermaphrodites now prefer to be called **intersexed**. Everybody ought to be called by names they've chosen. The earlier term carries painful baggage. Let's drop it.

taking place centuries and parsecs away from when and where they were written. Call this "Jetsons Syndrome." If you live in North America during the 21st century, avoid the worst effects of Jetsons Syndrome by taking notice of the time and place you're looking at, which are *not* universal, and which will affect your observations.

Another influence on your findings: what and who you're looking at. Nothing is simple, and difference is never going to be merely monolithic. Women are not merely women. Men are not merely men. Intersexes (aka *hermaphrodites*) are not merely intersexes. And so forth. On top of dealing with its nonbinary nature you want to remember that gender relates to and is influenced by race, age, physical ability, economic class, religious background, sexuality, and more. You have to take those factors into account.

While putting your research notes together, record the ways in which people you've studied are the same as your characters, and the ways they vary.

Aim for as many approaches to gathering information as possible. Maybe you won't be able to personally sneak a peek into a college football team's locker room for uncensored revelations on the behavior of 18- to 21-year-old males in that environment. If not, can you interview a college football player? That isn't exactly the same as being on the scene yourself, but it could help. Are there any books, blogs, or magazine articles about locker room atmosphere? Try to find them.

When considering gender-based differences in your characters, look for those that are less than obvious: the second-, third-, or even fourth-order implications of their gender. For instance, in a recent anthology edited by Mike Resnick, male authors were asked to write SF stories with female protagonists. Almost every plot centered on birth and pregnancy. This is an obvious, first-order implication of cisgendered womanhood: most women who are born female are fertile after adolescence and can give birth. Tobias Buckell extrapolated further; in "In the Heart of Kalikuata" he wrote about such women's need for a reliable method of birth control, and the impact of unwanted fertility on his protagonist's survival. Fertility implies a need for fertility control methods, so this was a second-order story. A third-order story might deal with the effects on its protagonist of a particular futuristic or magical means of birth control. A fourth-order story might deal with the social consequences of accepting or rejecting those effects.

This is work. Hopefully, it's work you enjoy doing.

Your how and your why

Scientific research has highlighted a number of differences in male and female brain size and organization, though there's recent evidence these differences may be exaggerated.** Sexual orientation seems to be determined before birth. Genetics almost certainly has an influence, but the uterine environment could also affect the matter.

Disentangling the roots of gender differences is an ongoing struggle, even when the biases mentioned above are adjusted for. How much of the gender variance we perceive after doing that is due to the effect of cultural norms? How much is owing to the global ubiquity of hormone-mimicking chemicals? How much is innate to our species? It's really difficult to figure those things out.

**See *Pink Brain, Blue Brain: How Small Differences Grow Into Troublesome Gaps—And What We Can Do About It* by Lise Eliot, Houghton Mifflin Harcourt, September, 2009, Boston, MA.

Despite all the open questions—or maybe because of them—the biology of gender provides an excellent base of material for speculative fiction. *Life* by Gwyneth Jones, winner of the 2004 Philip K. Dick Award, tells how researcher Anna Senoz discovers a mutation that erases secondary sexual characteristics, unbending several of gender's outward signifiers. In Samuel Delany's *Trouble on Triton*, switching bodies is easy for inhabitants of that Neptunian moon, and gender is an option, not an immutable fate. Numerous other novels and stories speculate on what could happen in similar circumstances. These are examples from science fiction, but the intersection of biology and gender comes into fantasy, too.

If you don't believe me, just ask yourself this: "Why should shapeshifters be barred from changing their gender as well as their species?"

As an author, you have to figure these things out. Maybe there's a cultural reason for shapeshifters sticking to their original gender. Maybe such a switch would be taboo. Or maybe it would be mandatory.

When you create a new society, whether in the future, on another planet, in a land beset by dragons, or on a plane of the afterlife, you have to structure how said society handles gender. And you will be doing a much more convincing job of building your world if you mention the higher-order implications of your decisions. Which divisions according to gender will remain in place when everyone gets equal pay for equal work? Which ones will become even more marked, and which ones will totally disappear?

Vive l'uniformité

People look for patterns, and in search of patterns we organize our experience into categories. We divide it up. We label the divisions and what they hold inside. We look for differences, and we see what we're looking for.

But sometimes in writing about gender it's a good idea to completely unbend it and focus only on similarities. Especially when you're representing human characters in the fantastic genres. Compared to robots and mermaids there are many traits humans of all genders have in common, many desires we share. We need to breathe air. We need water—fresh, sweet water—to drink. We need sleep.

Keep the differences you do need to depict in perspective.

Male lesbians, girlyboys, and honorary men

Of course, gender homogenization can go too far, just as gender variations can be blown up all out of proportion.

A male lesbian is a fictional construct; it's a label often claimed by a heterosexual man who is putting the moves on a woman. Lesbians want to have sex with women, see, and so does this horny man. Women, especially free-wheeling, liberated, modern women, shouldn't be fooled or put off by his maleness—a quality, by the way, that he has no intention of giving up.

Male lesbians are the pick-up line learning extension of a popular school of thought that instructs its students to write characters of differing genders just as they write those of their own. According to this curriculum, if I'm portraying a gay man all I need to do is inform my readers of this once or twice, then write about him as if writing about myself. Just go with what's natural. That method sounds easy, and it probably is. I've never tried it, having seen other authors' horrendous results.

Let's look at a couple of unpublished examples in order to save wear and tear on tender egos. Once upon a time, a never-to-be-named man in my critique group wrote a story from the point of view of a recently widowed woman in which she looked back on her first menstrual period. This man had no comparable experience, so he used his romanticized recollections of his own teen years as a template. The scene he came up with reminded me of an old Massengill commercial, with misty fields of daisies and drifting gauze. Another (female) member of the group assured him this was not the impression of their menarche most women of his character's background would have. A more accurate evocation of the memory would've involved cracked asphalt; a manhole cover engraved in an illegible script; warm, sweaty rain; and the blare of an approaching horn. And blood. There would definitely have been blood. Ah, yes, those were the days....

At another session of the same group, a man rejected a woman's depiction of her character's thought processes, which he said were those of a "girlyboy." Homosexual men are often described as behaving like straight women—though this is a clueless oversimplification—but the critiquer was saying that the author's man came across as too female rather than "too gay." The character was reflecting on a romantic relationship and doing it far more frequently than the reader deemed realistic.

Shifting our gaze from the anonymous to the common, we find that the appearance of girlyboys may be a special danger for romances intended for heterosexual women, including those of the paranormal variety. The hairless chests shown on some of their covers sort of give the show away, don't they? Like mystery writer Dorothy Sayers's creation Lord Peter Wimsey, SF girlyboys are appealing, but not exactly credible.

And then we come to the related phenomenon of characters who are men in all but name. Or in all but name and large breasts. Lara

Croft, for example. Honorary men like Lara kick all kinds of butt, mainly because they carry around big guns or wield humungous swords. Often they act out men's fantasies of aggression in ways designed to excite their sexual interest.

Swordswomen of the "honorary man" type are everywhere, and it's not hard to understand why. Start with the realization that most of us involved in the SF genre are outsiders. So outsider characters resonate with us. Add in a bit of history: In the past the large majority of people using swords have been men. Women who did so were a minority. Swordswomen have instant outsider status; they're instant geek magnets. But must they be glorified in contrast to and at the expense of female characters who embrace their assigned gender? Because when you do that, you can be read as devaluing a bunch of really cool attitudes, strategies, and experiences—such as cooperation and indirection—in favor of, say, violence and isolation.

When you're writing SF you'll find it helps to remain conscious of these tropes. Even if you don't manage to completely avoid them. Awareness is a powerful gender unbender.

At the time I write this there's one wonderful tool up online at

http://www.overthinkingit.com/wp-content/
uploads/2010/10/Overthinking-It-Female-Character-
Flowchart.png.

Enter that link in your browser and you'll see a gorgeous flowchart showing well-worn pathways to stereotyped female characters. Shana Mlawski and Carlos Hann Commander created it. There really ought to be several more of these to cover the various other gender stereotypes to be encountered in SF.

Specialties of the house

Okay, now let's *stop* assuming you want to write about humans. Or, at least, that you want to write about baseline humans, humans-as-we-know-them. Because this is SF, and we can do more. Your characters could be...

- Genetically, mechanically, or chemically modified humans with no genitals. Or two or more fully-functioning identical—or differing—sets of them. Anywhere on their bodies.
- Computer uploads of human descendants who give as much consideration to gender roles as we do to phrenology.
- Dryads without any reproductive mandate for assigning gender, who therefore base it on something else, such as the species of their host trees.
- Robots rebelling against the genders they've been assigned by human bosses.
- Ghosts whose physical basis for gender identity is gone.
- Aliens whose gender roles are based on reproductive biologies and cultures enormously different from Earth's.

If you're looking for resources to help you imagine those enormously different reproductive biologies, read *Dr. Tatiana's Sex Advice to All Creation* by Olivia Judson. In the guise of a sex columnist, Judson very helpfully gives us the skinny on a wide variety of nonhuman reproduction schemes. Also, it's funny.

Reading anthropological texts can stretch your capacity to

speculate about possible cultures, though some books reveal more about who wrote them than about their subjects. Laura Bohannon, Margaret Mead, and Alfred Kroeber are among the anthropologists I recommend.

Usually, though, you'll be modeling the gender of your nonhuman characters the same way you model the gender of your human characters: on people you're able to observe for yourself. In which cases you'll have to really, really, *really* pay attention to your perspective and built-in biases. Really.

Examples: The Good, the Bad, and the No You Didn't!

"Sexual Dimorphism," by Kim Stanley Robinson, examines an actual physical difference between genders and the possibility of some that are nonphysical. I've already mentioned Jones's *Life* and Delany's *Trouble on Triton* (originally published as *Triton*), and I'll add here that the rest of their oeuvres are equally rewarding showcases of how to approach gender in the fantastic genres. Nalo Hopkinson's *Midnight Robber* and Maureen McHugh's *Mission Child* both have wonderful things to say about the intersections of gender, culture, and race. Ursula K. Le Guin's *The Left Hand of Darkness* broke major fictional ground by introducing us to aliens whose gender regularly fluctuate. Any story by James Tiptree, Jr. will ring fascinating changes on gender assumptions, as will the stories and novels, which have won the award named after her, which was created in 1991. Winners of the Tiptree Award are listed online at http://tiptree.org/. For further reading consult the honors and long lists compiled for each year, available at that same Web site.

Bad examples? Let's keep this brief. Let's restrict it to authors no longer living, and to those otherwise respected for their work. Such as J.R.R. Tolkien, William Tenn, and Philip K. Dick. Tolkien's Middle

Earth is full of exclusively male wizards and essentialist elven ladies. In *Of Men and Monsters* Tenn describes a group of humans living as pests within the walls of an alien dwelling; his women characters lie to maintain their gender role as the community's cooks, despite new food supplies that don't need preparation. Dick's prescient conapts (today we call them condominiums) were inhabited by wage-slave husbands, and housewives unhappy with their futuristic appliances.

What we have here is a failure to fully envision gender. It's not good. But neither is it intentional.

There are books that do seem to want to validate traditionalist gender assumptions. In David Brin's post-apocalyptic novel *The Postman*, a rebellion against a misogynistic government is thwarted because a woman reveals the plot to a male lover. The message this imparts is that women can't be trusted with secrets, and that they're especially vulnerable to romantic blandishments.

Homework

- Sketch maps of gender, locating points for as many roles as you recognize.
- Look around you. Make notes on the gender roles you see and how they're enacted, what they mean. Consider your own prejudices and how they might affect what you observe. Consider the milieu in which you're conducting your observations and how that also might have an effect.
- Write up some generalizations about one or more genders. Then list several situations, locales, and times in which those generalizations may prove false.

- Pick your favorite observation about a gender you don't identify as your own. Extrapolate a second-order implication based on that observation. Extrapolate a third-order implication from the second-order one.
- Think about a gender you don't identify as your own. List everything you have in common with someone of that gender.
- Read at least one fiction and at least one nonfiction book mentioned above.
- Read *Writing the Other* by Nisi Shawl and Cynthia Ward and do all the exercises contained in it.
- Draft a character study of swordswoman who doesn't reject her society's version of her gender's values.
- Outline an SF plot in which an intersex person refuses to make a sacrifice of themself.
- Create your own individual list of SF novels and stories that you consider good, bad, and deliberately inflammatory works touching on gender.

Peptalk

Come on, unbend that gender. Figure out what it does and why and how. Deconstruct it. Fieldstrip it. Put it back together the way you want it to go.

Why? Because you can.

ALAN DEAN FOSTER

REVERSE ENGINEERING

Alan Dean Foster has written in a variety of genres, including hard science fiction, fantasy, horror, detective, western, historical, and contemporary fiction. He is also the author of numerous nonfiction articles on film, science, and scuba diving, as well as novelizations of several films, including Star Wars, the first three Alien films, Star Trek, and Transformers. His novel *Cyber Way* won the Southwest Book Award for Fiction in 1990, the first science fiction work ever to do so.

I didn't plan it.

Back in the Jurassic (1973), the vivacious and remarkable Judy-Lynn del Rey had just taken over editorship of the science fiction line at Ballantine Books. Someone had purchased the book rights to one of the worst films ever made, a dollop of stale Italian pasta called LUANA. As I was becoming known as a fast writer, and also happened to have an MFA in cinema from UCLA, she made the assumption that I knew my way around a film script. She asked if I would try writing a book based on LUANA'S screenplay. I said sure—and then found out that there was no screenplay. At least, not in English.

So a screening (16mm print, in a small room) was arranged for me at the distributor's offices in Hollywood. It was assumed that I would write the book based on a viewing of the film. The picture, of course, was entirely in unsubtitled Italian. It didn't matter: the film was an unqualified *tacchino* (that's Italian for turkey) of the first order.

What to do? The only sensible thing anyone associated with this mess of pottage did was to hire Frank Frazetta to do the advertising art. Frazetta promptly produced two gorgeous paintings of the eponymous jungle girl protagonist of the story flanked by a ferocious lion and giant black panther (yes, these paintings are reproduced in Frazetta's art books). So I novelized the paintings. Which is why the book is dedicated to Frazetta.

Postscript: After the book came out, a representative from Disney who had plainly neglected to read the fine print on the book covers contacted Judy-Lynn to inquire if the film rights to the book might be available. Both of us had a good laugh (and a good cry) over that one.

Lesson to be learned: If you know your profession, you should be able to make a good book out of *anything*. My second novelization job was the legendary John Carpenter/Dan O'Bannon student epic DARK STAR. Though infinitely better than LUANA in every cinematic way imaginable, DARK STAR is essentially about several guys sitting around in a starship talking about how bored they are. That was almost as difficult to get 70,000 words plus out of as LUANA.

After those two, every subsequent novelization I was asked to write seemed easy.

I'm frequently asked what makes a good novelization. That's simple—a good script. The better the original story, the better the end result. It's just like cooking. Fresh and interesting ingredients make for better food. Take ALIEN, the book version of which I wrote in three weeks while hunched over my prized IBM Selectric, mostly at night while looking over my shoulder. If the result scares me, I figure it should be able to scare readers. Or ALIENS, a completely different take on the same story, wherein some unnamed editorial genius at Warner Books figured they could enlarge their audience to include innocent adolescents by bowdlerizing all the Marine-speak in the book. An editorial decision for which my input was not solicited and at which I turned mildly apoplectic upon being confronted with the dismal fait accompli.

There was SHADOWKEEP, the first ever novelization of an original computer game. Writing it required me to tell the story without giving away any of the story elements. Do that and you don't have a novel—you have a game guide. That one wasn't easy either, especially since video gaming was in its infancy and unlike in today's games there were no real characters in the story—just tropes (hero, wizard, etc.) required to move the game forward.

Things were much better when I did my second and only other game novelization. THE DIG was based on an idea by the redoubtable Steven Spielberg, a director of some note, and produced by LucasArts, the game division of another moderately well-known director. Having vowed after SHADOWKEEP never to novelize another game again, I was taken in by THE DIG's premise. THE DIG isn't about interstellar warfare, it's not about swords and sorcerers, it's about—archeology. The idea was use the game not only for fun, but to inspire the players' interest in real science.

What a notion.

After LUANA and DARK STAR, Judy-Lynn asked if I would be willing to write a whole series of books based on the animated STAR TREK television series. Having zeroed-in on an exception in the contract between Bantam Books and Paramount that neglected to give Bantam the rights to animated adaptations of the franchise, she had promptly acquired said permissions. Again I acquiesced—only to discover that the scripts for the animated episodes were, unsurprisingly, each about twenty minutes long. Meaning twenty pages or so of teleplay.

I immediately informed Judy-Lynn that there was no way I was going to be able to get a full novel out of a twenty-page teleplay. "Do it the best way you can," she told me. So I hit upon the notion of expanding each teleplay into a novella and combining, as best I could, three such novellas into each book. This worked fine until one day I got a call from an excited JL.

"You've got four scripts left and you've got to get a full book out of each one!"

"Judy, I can't. I told you. If I could have done that I would have done it in the first place."

"I don't care," she admonished me. "You've got to get four more books out of the remaining scripts. Because the books are selling like crazy!"

Sooo... unable to expand a twenty-page teleplay into a full-length novel, I adapted each of the remaining four scripts into a novella just as I had with the others and then added two-thirds entirely original material to fill out each book. On the first of these (STAR TREK LOG SEVEN) I was able to utilize an unproduced screenplay I had written for the original Star Trek show. This was designed as a two-part episode. It was rejected by Norway Productions (Gene Roddenberry's production company), but I was asked to resubmit it "when we're picked up for next season." Which the show was not. But it made an excellent finishing two-thirds for the first of the expanded Log books. After that, I had to come up with new material to finish out the remaining three books. Fortunately, I had saved what I felt were the best two scripts for last. These were written by actual science fiction authors: Larry Niven and David Gerrold.

I've had the opportunity to novelize many of the major science fiction and fantasy films of the past thirty-five years. My work on STAR WARS came about because, I believe, someone connected to the film had read my original novel ICERIGGER and mentioned that it was similar in spirit to the film that was then in production. After it was determined that I might be a suitable candidate to do both the book version of the film as well as a sequel novel, I was asked to meet with George Lucas's lawyer. This was a test that I apparently passed, because he then arranged for me to meet with George.

The meeting took place at Lucas's nascent special effects facility, Industrial Light and Magic. At that time ILM occupied a rented warehouse in an industrial district of Van Nuys, part of greater Los Angeles, about five minutes drive from where I grew up. Arriving and parking, I walked past a series of flat plastic models that had been set up outside the building because they were too big to fit inside. These were the sections of Death Star surface that Luke Skywalker flies over in the climatic battle at the end of the film. At the time I had no idea what they were for, but the smell of glue was strong in the air.

While waiting inside for George I killed time chatting with John Dykstra, who proudly and enthusiastically showed me and attempted to explain to me his computer-controlled camera. I desperately feigned knowledge of what he was talking about. That day they were shooting the model of the Millenium Falcon. George arrived, energetically showed me around, presented the basketball-sized Death Star, and we conversed easily for as long as his time would allow. Prior to parting I asked him what he hoped to do if his film was something of a success.

"I'd like to do small experimental films," he told me.

Many years later, after considerably more films, in an interview on CBS's "60 Minutes," when asked what he wanted to do after all his successes, he said exactly the same thing. I hope the opportunity presents itself.

Different projects present different problems to the novelizer. On OUTLAND I remember trying to resolve the conundrum of how you justify the use of projectile weapons (i.e., ordinary guns) in an enclosed space on an airless moon, when one misplaced shot could rupture the outer wall and kill everyone busily engaged in the ongoing gun battle. On CLASH OF THE TITANS it was trying to resolve the actualities of Greek mythology with the cinematic aspirations of Ray Harryhausen, since Ray's visions often diverged from the Hellenic canon.

In the course of novelizing the screenplay I asked Harryhausen's long-time producer Charles Schneer why Ray didn't do something different. Lovecraft, for example. As a fan, I quietly thrilled at the prospect of a stop-motion Harryhausen Cthlulhu, Shuggoth, or Elder Gods.

"Oh," Charlie told me, "Ray won't do that. He just wants to do Greek and Roman mythology." He looked sad as he said it: a not uncommon expression among producers whose stars are hitched to powerful creative types.

It did not take long for me to realize and propound what I call the triple-S of Hollywood science fiction, and learn not to aggravate myself over it anymore than necessary. It is this:

Shot Supersedes Science.

No director I've met and talked with, no matter how famous or successful, will sacrifice something he or she wants to see on screen because it's bad science. It's this acquiescence to individual directorial vision that drives true science fiction fans and readers of the genre (as opposed to simply the viewers) to distraction. A good example would be Disney's THE BLACK HOLE, wherein we have giant flaming meteors rolling down the center of a starship, when in reality such a collision would result in total destruction of said vessel, and even people walking around in space without spacesuits (as Dave Barry would say, I am not making this up).

Or ALIEN 3, where c-cell powered flashlights are still the norm hundreds of years in the future. I'm sometimes asked why, after doing the book versions of ALIEN, ALIENS, and ALIEN 3, I didn't do the novelization of ALIEN RESURRECTION (i.e., Alien 4). The answer lies in ALIEN 3. After striving my best to correct errors of science, adjusting the plot to eliminate the obscenity of killing the little girl Newt, and providing detailed and realistic backgrounds for the participants (why they were sent to the film's prison planet in the first place), I received a letter from one of the producers, Walter Hill. In it I was told that I could not make such modifications, that I was required to write the book exactly as things were portrayed in the screenplay, and that the result would "we feel, make for a better book."

I did as I was told, taking out all the original material I had so laboriously crafted, and forbore from pointing out that I had done this sort of thing before and had some small success with it.

Readers must understand that a novelization is a work for hire. It is neither owned nor controlled by the writer. As a house painter, if the homeowner says they want their dwelling painted chartreuse and pink, you suck down your objections and paint it chartreuse and pink. If there's one thing I've learned while working on films produced or directed by some of Hollywood's biggest names, it's that the most confident will listen to and take advice from anyone.

Even janitors. Even animal wranglers. And yes, even writers. George Lucas is a prime example of someone who's willing to listen. So was Alan Ladd, Jr. There are others, but they are rarer than you might imagine. After seeing some of what passes for science fiction on the big screen, most true aficionados of the genre (meaning those who actually read books) already know this.

Once, I was granted the opportunity to novelize a fine film that's neither science fiction nor fantasy—or is it? I refer to the Clint Eastwood western PALE RIDER. The principles of making such a script into a novel remain the same regardless of subject matter. Expand upon the action. Get into the characters' heads to reveal what they're thinking. Describe scenes in far more detail. Add new material that expands upon the screenwriter's work without contradicting it.

At the end of the film Eastwood's character rides off into the distance and at the very last instant, seems to vanish. I emphasized this moment as strongly as I could, feeling that it solidified the fantasy aspect of the story in ways the film itself tends to gloss over. Sometimes, if you're subtle enough and the studio is sufficiently indifferent to what you are doing, you are allowed to embolden elements that leap out at you. You can only hope they also exist, unfulfilled, in the screenwriter's mind. Sometimes you can do something notable. And sometimes you can miss the intent entirely, overcome by your own perceptions.

I read Richard Matheson's short story DUEL when it first appeared in Playboy magazine. Many years after seeing the film version of the story made for TV that constituted Steven Spielberg's real breakthrough, I had the opportunity to chat with Richard about something that had bothered me ever since the film had first appeared.

"It's too bad the film shows the truck driver's legs in a couple of shots," I told Richard, proud of my powers of observation. "If not for that, then you maintain the feeling that there's no one in the truck and that it's embarked an inimical mission of its own. It makes a classic fantasy film into an ordinary chase story."

"Oh," replied Richard, "I always envisioned there being a driver in the truck."

Eeeeowww... that whining sound you hear is Mr. Perspicacious going down in flames.

But I *still* think it works better if the viewer doesn't see the driver's legs.

That's the kind of detail a novelizer needs to be careful to clear with the original screenwriters. You can expand upon, you can modify, you can elaborate, but you cannot do anything that changes the original out of recognition.

Not long ago I found myself in the position of having to novelize three major films at virtually the same time—the latest STAR TREK, TRANSFORMERS: REVENGE OF THE FALLEN, and TERMINATOR SALVATION. Plus write an original bridge novel linking the two TRANSFORMER films. It was moderately insane, but fun. Why? Because I'm basically a fan. Essentially still that fourteen-year old kid sitting in the back of the theater with his friends munching popcorn while loudly criticizing the crummy special effects. Only with better word skills.

You can't do a good job turning a screenplay into a novel unless you're a fan. Writing skills aren't enough. With a good film, you bring enthusiasm to the work. With a bad one (KRULL, say, with its schizoid inability to ever decide if it's science fiction or fantasy) you bring even more enthusiasm. The same kind of enthusiasm expressed by those now more-knowledgeable-than-ever teens who know BS when they see it and who will twitter a film to death if they feel they're being talked down to. Me, I never talk down to the reader in either my original work *or* my novelizations.

Because I remember how it was.

ALETHEA KONTIS

KEVIN J. ANDERSON TALKS ABOUT SPIN-OFFS, PREQUELS, AND FAN FICTION

Alethea Kontis is the author of children's picture books *AlphaOops: The Day Z Went First* and *H Is for Halloween*. She shares credit for *The Dark-Hunter Companion* with Sherrilyn Kenyon, whose Dark-Hunter series the *Companion* documents. She co-edited the 2006 science fiction and fantasy anthology *Elemental*, a benefit anthology for children who survived the 2004 Indian Ocean tsunami.

Kevin J. Anderson has written spin-off novels for *Star Wars*, *StarCraft*, *Titan A.E.*, and *The X-Files*, and with Brian Herbert is the co-author of the *Dune* prequels. His original works include the *Saga of Seven Suns* series and the Nebula Award-nominated *Assemblers of Infinity*. He has also written several comic books including the Dark Horse *Star Wars* collection *Tales of the Jedi* written in collaboration with Tom Veitch, Predator titles (also for Dark Horse), and X-Files titles for Topps. Some of Anderson's superhero novels include *Enemies & Allies*, about the first meeting of Batman and Superman and *The Last Days of Krypton*, telling the story of how Krypton came to be destroyed and the choice two parents had to make for their son.

Alethea Kontis: In your words, please define intellectual property *and* fan fiction, *and how the two are often confused.*

Kevin J. Anderson: Both are based on an existing property or universe (Star Wars, Star Trek, etc.) that is owned by someone other than the author. *Fan fiction* is written by authors who don't have the permission of the copyright holder or owner of the intellectual property—Star Wars fiction written without the sanction of Disney, for example, which now owns Star Wars. In authorized media tie-in fiction, the author is working with the full knowledge and permission of the creator or copyright owner.

Kontis: How does an interested writer get involved in writing for a certain intellectual property?

Anderson: The process is straightforward, but in most cases aspiring authors don't like the process. In order to be chosen to write for a certain intellectual property, a writer first has to establish himself as a successful, talented writer in his own right. Write your own stuff—once you've proved that you've got the skills to produce professional-caliber, publishable work, then you have passed the first step of the job audition. And then you start asking people, meeting editors, joining writers' organizations, and keep looking for openings.

Too many writers want to waltz in and be chosen to write for Star Wars, without ever proving that they can write a publishable short story, without demonstrating that they can even write a novel-length manuscript. Nobody ever said it would be easy.

Kontis: To date, how many intellectual properties have you written for?

Anderson: More than a dozen. I'm probably forgetting some.

Kontis: What was the first IP you wrote for? How were you approached?

Anderson: Star Wars. I didn't go looking at all, just concentrated on writing my own books, turned them in on time, worked well with the editors, attended a lot of science fiction conventions (so my enthusiasm for the genre was plain). But my editors were watching; they liked working with me, knew I was reliable, and when Lucasfilm (the owner of the franchise at that time) asked for author suggestions for future Star Wars projects, my name came up. The phone call came from out of the blue.

Kontis: What are the biggest advantages of working with an IP?

Anderson: You are dealing with familiar characters and settings, a series that the reader already loves before she even reads page one of your book. And I only work on properties that I already enjoy as a fan, so it's a lot of fun.

Kontis: What are some of the biggest challenges working with an IP?

Anderson: Working with a lot of approvals, other licensors, people who ask for changes in the story not for any plot reason, but because something in the chapter doesn't work with a new action-figure design in production. And, if it's a complex property with a lot of history, just keeping track of all the background material and established stories can become a huge chore.

KEVIN J. ANDERSON TALKS ABOUT SPIN-OFFS, PREQUELS, AND FAN FICTION

Kontis: What are some mistakes that writers of IP commonly make?

Anderson: They forget that it's not *theirs*—you are a gun for hire, a person who is allowed to play with the cool toys in the sandbox, but you don't get to keep them. They are owned by someone else.

Kontis: Does the publisher of the IP provide you with a bible of information you have to follow, or are you expected to already be familiar with the material?

Anderson: Yes. No. Both. Keep in mind that every IP is different. Some have dedicated staff to monitor all the different properties being licensed, continuity experts, libraries with all the background. Other IPs are new and growing and, frankly, everybody's making it up as they go along.

Kontis: What are some things to look for in IP contracts that might be different from normal contracts?

Anderson: First, expect the terms to be a lot more draconian. You don't *own* anything. You are doing work for hire, and the IP holder has the right to change—or force you to change—whatever they want. Royalties are usually very low, and sometimes there are no royalties at all. You are usually paid well up front, but you won't have the copyright in your work. That's just the way it is.

Kontis: You write both IP material and your own original series. Are there any processes you do differently or environments you change when writing each? For instance, do you hike while working on an IP and hang-glide when doing original material?

Anderson: I love them both. I have a great many fans who came to my original work because they recognized me for something I did in a series they already enjoyed. I don't have a different process or treat the two types of work differently—i.e., I don't put in any less work because something is "only" a media tie-in project. For my current epic fantasy series, an original work, I did a lot of research in historical sailing ships and maritime legends; for my Dune books with Brian Herbert I do just as much research on politics, ecology, astronomy, and also I immerse myself in Frank Herbert's original Dune series.

Kontis: *Are there special associations for or awards given to writers of tie-in media?*

Anderson: The International Association of Media Tie-In Writers is the only organization I know of for this specialized field (yes, I'm a member). They give out an annual series of awards, the Scribes, for work in the field of media tie-ins.

Kontis: *Is there an IP out there that you haven't written for yet but wish you could?*

Anderson: Hmm, I've already made some phone calls....

ELIZABETH BEAR

TACTICS OF WORLDBUILDING

Elizabeth Bear was a winner of the 2005 John W. Campbell Award for Best New Writer, the 2008 Hugo Award for Best Short Story for "Tideline," and the 2009 Hugo Award for Best Novelette for "Shoggoths in Bloom." She is one of only five writers who have gone on to win multiple Hugo Awards for fiction after winning the John W. Campbell Award for Best New Writer.

The term *worldbuilding*, as it's commonly bandied about, covers two distinct auctorial activities. One of them is designing the world, making it consistent and relevant and quirky and fascinating. And the other is somehow transferring that information into the reader's brain, so that said reader feels as if this—perhaps foreign and wondrous—place is as solid and real as Venezuela. That is to say, someplace unfamiliar, but accessible. Someplace with its own fabric of history and culture. (If you happen to live in Venezuela, please substitute Boston, above.)

It might seem that this is a skill that's only necessary to those of us writing in alternate or alien worlds—as exemplified by so-called *second-world fantasy*. But it turns out that this attention to detail is even more essential in fantastic fiction based on our own world, where readers are likely to treat every inconsistency as an intentional bread-crumb laid by the writer to lead them to the resolution of some vital narrative mystery.

The good news is there are a whole bunch of proven worldbuilding techniques that, with practice, you can use to make your settings seem like places that breathe. What follows is not meant to be an exhaustive list—I doubt that's possible—but simply an overview of possibilities.

First and perhaps most important is **research**. Too often, speculative fiction authors rely on what's common knowledge, or worse, reap from what they've read in other fictional treatments of a topic. This leads pretty quickly to something called *the third-artist problem*. In other words, the first artist draws his inspiration from life. The second artist enters into a conversation with the first artist. And the third artist merely copies slavishly what the first two have said, without understanding why any of it happened that way.

As an example of this, consider the innumerable imitators of Tolkien who have peopled their fantasy worlds with elves, dwarves, and orcs without ever pausing to consider what structural and thematic purposes those races serve in the original work—and without ever pausing to read the original Norse and Anglo-Saxon narratives from which Tolkien drew his inspiration.

There are other critical quibbles with Tolkien, but few people fault his worldbuilding. It's possible that Tolkien lavished more attention and love on Middle-Earth than any author before or since in developing a fantastic setting. Any single one of the Middle Earth cultures contains the detail most modern authors would spread over an entire series of books.

This is fitting. Tolkien's masterpiece is not *The Lord of the Rings* and ancillary texts. It's Middle-Earth itself, and his five novels are merely a fortunate byproduct of that passion. Reproducing that is not so simple as sketching a suspiciously rectangular map of Fantasyland and sprinkling it with forests and mountain ranges.

Fortunately, as writers, we are not required to duplicate it. (I say fortunately, because for very few of us these days would it be possible to forge a career out of five novels.) What we are required to do, however, is to give the audience the sense that the world they visit is real, that it's bigger around the edges than what is shown in the story.

One way to do that is through research and creation rather than imitation. If we draw our inspiration from the real world rather than fictional ones, we're more likely to come up with something new and interesting as opposed to something banal and predictable.

As an example, in *A Companion to Wolves* and its sequels, the Norse fantasies I wrote with Sarah Monette, I found myself using a lot of the same original source material Tolkien did—the Eddas and Sagas, specifically. While we declined to name any dwarves Balin and Bombur, we did use elves. Or alfar, to use the term appropriate to the milieu. Specifically, svartalfar, the *black elves*, a race not mentioned in Tolkien.

We had great fun with them, inventing a culture very different from (and in all honesty considerably more shallow than) that of Tolkien's elves, but as useful to our narrative.

This applies to everything. Want to write about werewolves? Read nonfiction—preferably original sources!—that discusses werewolves, rather than a fistful of werewolf novels that may all be copying each other and *The Wolf Man*. Want to write in the Elizabethan period? By all means, go to original sources, and the many histories and biographies of the time. Want to write in a setting that's less well-documented, or perhaps not documented in a language you are familiar with? The best choice there is to read scholarly works on the period—and read a lot of them, not just one or two—so you can come to your own conclusions about the time.

Your mastery of the topic will shine through in your writing, even though you will—of course—be wise enough to avoid extensive and boring infodumps that basically amount to recounting your research without moving the narrative forward.

The skilled writer of speculative fiction remembers that every sentence performs at least two and preferably three of the following four tasks: creating or resolving tension (i.e., asking or answering questions that move the plot forward); developing theme; illuminating character; and building the world.

The more firmly the writer knows her own world, the more mastery and confidence she will show in answering the inevitable questions the setting throws at her. Confidence is essential: The reader can tell when you don't have it. Your authority as a narrator flags, and he starts looking around for the holes in the plot.

Which leads us to the next point. In addition to **research**, another of the writer's most effective tactics for worldbuilding is entirely internal and takes place well before pen meets page. It is the fine art of **asking the third question**, and I wish more writers were aware of it.

To wit: good worldbuilding is more than one question deep, even though the narrative itself may only go one question into an explanation. For example, say we have a volcano in an unlikely place. The narrative may explain to us that that volcano is there because a Dark God punched a hole in the earth's crust when he was flung to earth by the Fluffy Bunnies of the Apocalypse, allowing magma to flow free. The author should know—because inevitably an interviewer will ask—how it was that he came to be flung to earth in that place, or what the sequence of events leading up to his fall was. But the author should also know, for her own use, at least in general terms, what was there before the volcano, how the volcano affected local trade routes, and so on.

A good example of this occurs in Anne McCaffery's early Pern novels. She mentions, several times, in passing, that an inactive volcano has become active again, and this is a traditional sign of impending danger from the rapacious substance known as *thread*. What she does not mention, but obviously knows, is that this volcano starts smoking because the approach of the Red Star that also heralds the arrival of thread is messing with Pern's tectonic integrity. Why? Well, because the Red Star is an erratic planet, and it exerts a tidal pull on Pern. Why? Well, the thread is a spore that actually travels across space *from* the Red Star, which is why these three events are linked.

And so on.

By **asking the third question**, the writer assures herself that she has thought through the reader's basic objections, and is writing in such a way that the implications of what she writes will suggest an explanation. Failure to do this can lead to awkwardness when the reader realizes that if (as the narrative maintains) every elvish woman in the story can only have one child in her lifetime, and yet the elves are not in danger of dying out, and they are also not immortal...

Something is wrong with the math.

It's a simple matter of thinking things through. If your fantasy world has had entirely static governments and technology level for the past thousand years, *why*? Your reader is surely aware that this is an unnatural state of affairs. It behooves the author to be aware of that, too. If your world has supernatural monsters and yet nobody is aware of them, why not? If they *are* aware of them, what changes has their existence wrought upon society? (Robin McKinley's *Sunshine* is a very nice take on this.)

Both of these tactics rely heavily on consistency. The author needs to understand her world so she can set it out clearly for the reader so that when contradictions arise, they are intentional and clue the reader into mysteries that need resolving.

Another thing to consider, once you've dispensed with the logical structures of your world, is how to make it innovative. One cannot too much overestimate the usefulness of plain old awesome—wild, rampant **creativity**—in selling a world to an audience. Cool stuff is *very* important, and the cooler your stuff and the faster your narrative is moving, the more likely readers will be to forget the inevitable failures of consistency—if they even notice them. A happy reader will patch your story for you. One of the greatest strengths writers of fantastic fiction have is that our readers are pattern and inference *machines*. Our brains are designed to figure stuff out from insufficient clues. So by providing just enough clues—and giving the reader space to do the inventing— the reader may come up with a cooler scenario than the author ever imagined.

Which leads us to our last technique of this section: don't **overexplain**. For one thing, it's boring. For another, once you start explaining, the reader slows down and starts trying to find answers to everything. And the writer will inevitably fail that test. So the trick is to explain just enough, and let the reader have enough information to make some helpful inferences.

Only experience and practice can really determine how much explanation is enough, and how much is too much.

All of these techniques apply *before* the writer sets pen to page. There are also a number that apply *while* she is writing—specifically, these are **tactics of exposition**.

First among these, of course, is the venerable **infodump**, or *expositional lump*. Oft-reviled, the infodump used artfully is nevertheless one of the best means of delivering information to the reader.

But the key here is artfulness. Specifically, a good infodump must be just as fascinating to the reader as any other part of the narrative. This requires the author to acquire the skills of a good nonfiction writer as well as a good storyteller. This may surprise some, but excellence in nonfiction requires many of the same skills that excellence in fiction does—wit, narrative energy, clarity, and the ability to generate and resolve tension.

Second among these tactics is the art of **in-line exposition**—of delivering nuggets of necessary data in the flow of the narrative without disrupting it, of clarifying or defining an issue as soon as it arises. For example, when the author first uses a foreign word, she can define it in a phrase. She can introduce information the same way she'd mention the color of a character's eyes or hair. When the information is part of the flow of the narrative, the reader consumes it like chewable vitamins: it doesn't seem like medicine when it's going down.

This tactic leads inexorably to a technique for which author Jo Walton has coined the useful term **incluing**, which she defines as "scattering pieces of information seamlessly through the text to add up to a big picture." It may help the novice or journeyman writer to consider this in terms of how the writers of whodunits scatter clues through their text that are meant to seem invisible until picked out by the detective at the end, at which point they amount to a foolproof blueprint to the identity of the evildoer.

In the case of speculative fiction, however, the "detective" is the reader, and the "evildoer" is the nature of the world we're moving through.

This is an outgrowth of the art of implication, where the writer leaves open an inevitable conclusion, allowing the reader to fill it in. This—and incluing—are slightly dirty tricks, because any time the reader convinces himself of something by inference or deduction, he will be far more dedicated to that belief than if the author simply told him. It's a good way to get the reader on your side, in other words, but it can backfire badly when the reader deduces something that you absolutely did not want him to believe.

This is why it's vitally important to have control of your worldbuilding.

While we're on recently coined words for age-old tactics, the final technique I'd like to mention is one that my writing group calls **inpositioning.** This is the simple tactic of the writer taking as unquestioned truth the basic tenets of her worldbuilding and writing as if there were no question about their truth. This tactic requires confidence and narrative authority, but when done right it is utterly seamless and elegant. I used a lot of this technique in my *other* Norse fantasy world, starting with *All the Windwracked Stars*, in which I was attempting to present a world where the dominant European culture derived not from Christianity but from the old Norse religions, which had survived as a primary cultural force into a twenty-second century level of technology. The trappings of the society aren't all that different from any cyberpunk world— but its philosophical underpinnings are not predicated on ideals of meekness and forgiveness.

It was an interesting experiment.

In any case, this is how worlds get built: with meticulous care, wild creativity, rigorous logic, and a good deal of bald-faced courage.

JACKIE GAMBER

ANN VANDERMEER TALKS
ABOUT WEIRD FICTION

Jackie Gamber is an award-winning editor and writer of genre-bending science fiction, fantasy, horror, and paranormal short stories, novels, and screenplays. She is a member of Science Fiction Writers of America and Horror Writers Association. She was named honorable mention in L. Ron Hubbard's Writers of the Future Award and is a winner of the Mary Shelley Award for Imaginative Fiction. In addition, during Jackie's tenure as executive editor of Meadowhawk Press, the indie house captured Science Fiction's Philip K. Dick Award, only the fourth time in history the award has gone to a small press. She is also writer/director of Allotrope Media, an indie film studio established for short film adaptations and tie-ins to literary projects.

Ann VanderMeer is a Hugo award-winning editor and publisher. From 2007-2011 she was fiction editor of Weird Tales, the oldest fantasy magazine in the U.S. She has edited the Best American Fantasy series as well as numerous other anthologies, including The Thackery T. Lambshead Cabinet of Curiosities, Steampunk, *and* Fast Ships, Black Sails. She is the founder of Buzzcity Press. Upon leaving Weird Tales, Ann founded The Weird Fiction

Review with her husband Jeff VanderMeer. Recently (along with Jeff VanderMeer) she edited the epic anthology The Weird, a massive survey of weird fiction from across multiple genres that won the 2012 British Fantasy Award. She currently serves as Contributing Fiction Editor for Tor.com.

Jackie Gamber: Historically, the term weird fiction *was used as a subgenre of speculative fiction around the late 1800s to early 1900s, and continued in literary venues even as the science fiction pulp magazines soared in popularity. What do you see as the hallmarks of weird fiction at that time?*

Ann VanderMeer: Weird fiction is a label attached to certain types of supernatural fiction, not to be confused with ghost stories, which were very popular at that time. There's something in the way the main characters react in a weird story, which points to *something beyond*, something that cannot be identified. It's the desire to seek out answers and to understand the unknown and perhaps even the unknowable. This quality of something *other* comes through the pages. But not in a traditional sense, such as with ghosts, vampires, etc. These stories on the whole don't give easy answers or the usual answers for what's happening (or may not give any answers at all). The characters are not necessarily going to get out of the nightmare, or even recognize they were in a nightmare from the beginning.

Gamber: Which authors of the time would you say had the most influence in the genre, and why?

VanderMeer: If you are talking about late 1800s early 1900s, the most well-known name here would be H.P. Lovecraft, whose Cthulhu mythos still endure as an influence on fiction, movies, video games, and most all popular culture pastimes today. Other writers include Arthur Machen, who blended supernatural rituals and horror with veiled sexuality (a subject that would send Lovecraft screaming out of the room). Algernon Blackwood introduced the world to some of the most horrifying stories of that time that were based more in the natural world, rather than elements from the outside. And that is precisely what made them all the more horrific, because as a reader, you think you know the way the world works and when you find that you do not, it's pretty unsettling. Lord Dunsany had a way to blending fantasy worlds and creatures into our world, and his work was a great influence on Lovecraft, actually.

Gamber: H.P. Lovecraft has been credited with adopting the term, and attempting to define it, in his essay Supernatural Horror in Fiction. *In the essay (to mixed reviews) he claims that in weird works "Atmosphere is the all-important thing" and that in a tale where horror is "... finally explained away by natural means, is not a genuine tale of cosmic fear". Do you see this as a valid description of weird fiction as a whole, or more a description of Lovecraft's writing in particular?*

VanderMeer: I have to agree about the explaining part. If you know what it is in the end, it's not a 'weird' tale. Maybe it's a ghost or a nuclear attack or a serial killer or what have you. Weird tales don't necessary have to scare you, it's not about the scare. It is more about the feeling of discomfort. A quiet, perhaps even suppressed scream, if you will, once you realize you are in the middle of a nightmare and can't wake up.

Gamber: How do you see Lovecraft's definition of weird fiction differing from that of horror?

VanderMeer: Weird fiction is more about seeking answers to the unanswerable questions. And it can be more subtle, the fear can creep up on you. Horror fiction has got to have the scare, the terror. As I described this difference once on a panel: Horror is that shock to the system, the in-your-face, blood-and-guts kind of scare. You can't ignore it. Weird is more like a gentle tap on your shoulder, when you turn around and see nothing there, but you know, you just know something is there. You just don't know what it is.

Gamber: Do you see weird fiction as veering away from the boom of science fiction in the 1950s to evolve toward its own genre? Or do you think cross-pollinating began in those early magazines?

VanderMeer: I believe it is its own genre and has been for quite some time. The cross-pollination had more to do with the stories being collected together in the same magazine, more than the work itself having elements of both, especially in the early part of the last century.

Today you are seeing much more mixing within the stories themselves and writers are influenced by so many things. You have to keep in mind that Lovecraft presented the Cthulhu Elder Gods to the world almost 100 years ago, but today you see other talented writers use this one theme for all kinds of fiction and art, not always weird. Take a look at George R.R. Martin's "Sandkings." This is a perfect example of a science fiction story that is truly weird. It's not just science fiction. But it's certainly not a traditional weird tale either.

Gamber: Weird Tales *magazine, first founded in 1923, boasts the launch of several writers' careers, including Lovecraft, as well as popularizing such writers as C.M. Eddy, Robert Bloch, Ray Bradbury, Robert E. Howard. At the time, the magazine's ambition was to publish writing so strange and fantastic that it couldn't be printed anywhere else. Considering that some of the early stories, such as the tales of Conan the Barbarian, could neatly fit under more modern subgenres today, such as sword and sorcery or soft science fiction, do you think the concept of what was weird back then has changed in comparison to what is considered weird now?*

VanderMeer: Yes, I do. All those subgenres of subgenres were brand new and didn't fit into any easy classification of what was being published in the pulp magazines back then. At the time *Weird Tales* was the haven for those stories. But out of that haven grew certain real genres, such as S&S and weird fiction. We've had weird fiction before *Weird Tales* magazine; we just didn't call it that. As Stephen Segal (my co-conspirator in *Weird Tales*) has said, *Weird Tales* was the place where two storytelling concepts met: *speculative* and *alternative*. In 1923, when the magazine was founded, those two ideas amounted to the same thing. *Weird Tales* was explicitly launched as a vehicle for writers trying to publish stories that were so bizarre and far out, other magazines refused to buy them—and those stories fell into two categories: tales of supernatural occurrences and tales of future worlds. The phrase *science fiction* wouldn't be coined for several years yet, but right from the start, the early editors of *Weird Tales* were not only publishing it, they understood perfectly well that it was just the newest face of the fantastic literary tradition that stretched from Homer to Shakespeare to Shelley and Poe and Verne.

Gamber: *Do you think the development of so many speculative fiction subgenres has effectively watered down the concept of weird fiction, or has it highlighted its uniqueness?*

VanderMeer: No, I don't think subgenres water anything down. I think the various styles of storytelling, the mixing and matching of genres, only helps to bring freshness to what some might think are tired old ideas and all-too-familiar takes. I love the idea that writers today have influences that stretch back to classic fiction such as Edgar Allen Poe and M.R. James (and even earlier) and yet are also influenced by today's video games and movies.

It was interesting as Jeff [VanderMeer] and I were putting together *The Weird*, we looked at early influences of the writers. We found that many writers in more contemporary times were actually writing fan fiction, of a sort, to the master of earlier days. So when we realized it, we went back to the source and found fiction that was stronger, more unique and unusual and yet still relevant (and readable) today. It was very important that each story we selected could still be read and enjoyed by a modern audience. Not all the earlier tales had that timeless quality. Not even all the stories we read from the '70s and '80s had that quality, so we passed over a lot of what others thought were classics of that time. Too many cultural references and in-jokes will keep a story from becoming a true classic.

Gamber: Weird Tales *magazine has gone through several incarnations since it first ceased publication in 1954, including some reprint anthologies and original novels, to a rebirth in 1988 as a serial publication with such authors as Tanith Lee and Nina Kiriki Hoffman. While you were serving as the magazine's fiction editor,* Weird Tales *won its first-ever Hugo award in 2009. Do you think the progression of the magazine parallels the evolution of the genre itself?*

VanderMeer: I think the magazine displays clearly the preferences and choices of whoever the editor is at that time. Under my editorship, my goal was to take the heart, soul, and spirit of the magazine and move it into the 21st century. Along with a lot of very talented people, including Stephen H. Segal, I was able to do just that, as evidenced by the first ever Hugo nomination and subsequent win. What I didn't want to do was move the magazine back to the "good old days" of pulp fiction. Keep in mind that the original goal of the magazine was to publish the new, unusual, and unique stories of *that day*. My vision was the same, but I was doing it in 2009, not 1923.

Gamber: For writers today looking to advance a career in weird fiction, what would you say would be the hallmark of weird stories in comparison to our modern understanding of other genres, such as space opera, psychological horror, bizarro, or urban fantasy?

VanderMeer: I am a firm believer in letting writers write whatever the heck they want to write and not worry about labels or genres. The minute they start worrying about that, the story suffers. They shouldn't even think about markets, not until the story is done and they need to figure out where to send it. Write the story you want to write. That's about the best advice I can give.

I remember reading a story from a young writer at a workshop. It was a beautiful story about a son coming to grips with his strained relationship with his father and—bam!—right in the middle of the story, there's a witch. This came out of nowhere. When I asked the writer about it, he said he purposefully added this character because this was a 'fantasy' workshop and he thought he'd take a perfectly good mainstream story and tack on a fantasy element. Needless to say, this didn't work. He ruined the story. I wonder if he ever went back to his original vision.

Gamber: *Do you see a place for weird fiction as science fiction and fantasy continue to evolve and cross over into mainstream literature?*

VanderMeer: Yes, people will always be drawn to and intrigued by the weird tale, whether it was written over 100 years ago or yesterday. Because as humans we will always be seeking the answers to the big philosophical questions. Although reading weird fiction isn't necessarily a religious experience, you can certainly see the spiritual appeal for something so supernatural and inexplicable.

Gamber: *What fresh vision can* new weird *bring to the tradition of weird fiction?*

VanderMeer: I am not really sure it can. It's something different altogether. The term *new weird* was tagged to the unclassifiable dark fiction that was being published in the early 2000s. It was M. John Harrison that coined the term and he ascribed it to the work of China Mieville, Steph Swanston, Jeff VanderMeer, and other writers at that time. New weird has been defined as a subgenre, which merges elements of science fiction, fantasy, and horror, while being written in a literary prose style. The way I see it, it's almost like what the New Wave subgenre did with traditional science fiction in *New Worlds* magazine, under the editorship of Michael

Moorcock. New weird is similar but from the horror point of view, rather than SF.

Gamber: What is your recommended book list for writers, new and established, in order to read the best of what weird fiction has to offer?

VanderMeer: OK, this is a leading question. Of course I am going to mention *The Weird*, which I edited with my husband [Jeff VanderMeer]. It spans over 100 years, includes 116 stories that represent over 100 writers from 20 countries in 1200 pages (almost one million words of fiction). We searched far and wide to make it inclusive, and yet at the same time, we worked to rectify past slights by including work that others might not have seen as weird at first glance. We also contracted seven new translations for stories that were first translated in the '50s and '60s. Those translations needed to be updated, so the stories would read well to a contemporary audience. In addition, we have another story that is translated into English for the first time. I recommend this book as great starting point. The writers in the book will lead you to other writers and other stories.

SHORT FICTION: A ROUNDTABLE DISCUSSION WITH SHORT STORY EDITORS

MODERATED BY MICHAEL KNOST

Michael Knost is an author, editor, and columnist of science fiction, fantasy, horror, and supernatural thrillers. He has written many books in various genres, helmed several anthologies, as well as nonfiction projects such as his Bram Stoker Award-winning book *Writers Workshop of Horror*. He has also served as ghostwriter for several projects, including associations with the *Discovery Channel* and *Lionsgate Media*. To find out more, visit www. MichaelKnost.com.

John Joseph Adams is the editor of several speculative fiction anthologies. He worked as assistant editor at *The Magazine of Fantasy & Science Fiction* before leaving in 2010 to edit *Lightspeed Magazine,* an online science fiction magazine, and then in March 2011 he took charge of its sister publication, *Fantasy Magazine.*

Ellen Datlow is a multiple award-winning editor who has been editing science fiction, fantasy, and horror short fiction for almost thirty years. She was fiction editor of *OMNI Magazine* and *SCIFICTION* and has edited more than fifty anthologies, including the horror half of the long-running *The Year's Best Fantasy and Horror,* and is now editing *The Best Horror of the Year* published by Night Shade Books.

James Patrick Kelly's fiction has been translated into sixteen languages. In 2007 he won the Nebula Award, given by the Science Fiction Writers of America, for his novella "Burn" and the World Science Fiction Society's Hugo Award twice: in 1996, for his novelette "Think Like a Dinosaur" and in 2000, for his novelette, "Ten to the Sixteenth to One." He writes a column on the internet for *Asimov's Science Fiction Magazine* and has two podcasts: Free Reads and James Patrick Kelly's StoryPod.

Mike Resnick co-edits *Jim Baen's Universe.* He has 5 Hugo Awards and other awards in the USA, France, Japan, Spain, Croatia, and Poland. As of 2007, he is first on the *Locus* list of all-time award winners, living or dead, for short fiction, and fourth on the Locus list of science fiction's all-time top award winners in all fiction categories.

Stanley Schmidt has contributed numerous stories and articles to original anthologies and magazines, including *Analog, Asimov's, The Magazine of Fantasy & Science Fiction, Rigel, The Twilight Zone, Alfred Hitchcock's Mystery Magazine,*

SHORT FICTION: A ROUNDTABLE DISCUSSION
WITH SHORT STORY EDITORS

American Journal of Physics, Camping Journal, Writer's Digest, and *The Writer.* He has edited or coedited about a dozen anthologies, and recently retired as the fiction editor at *Analog Science Fiction and Fact.*

Gordon Van Gelder is a Hugo Award-winning American science fiction editor. He is both editor and publisher of *The Magazine of Fantasy & Science Fiction,* for which he has twice won the Hugo Award for Best Editor Short Form. He was also a managing editor of *The New York Review of Science Fiction* from 1988 to 1993.

Michael Knost: What influence, if any, do cover page publishing credits have in regard to your decision of acceptance or rejection?

John Joseph Adams: I would say it has zero influence. Having authors submit who have previously published stories is always great, and having other professional publications might make me take a harder look at something before passing on it, but ultimately it has no effect in whether or not I accept something for publication. The story has to stand on its own merits, regardless of what other fine work the author may have produced. Though I guess if I was on the fence about whether or not to accept something, the fact that an author has lots of previous publications (and so may have a fanbase) might help me decide. I've certainly had well-known authors submit stories to me—authors that I'd love to have in my magazines—that I had to reject because they just didn't work for me, or they just didn't fit my vision for the type of fantasy or science fiction I'm going for in the magazines.

One thing that factors in is whether or not a submission is

unsolicited, or if I asked the writer to send something to me. If I specifically requested a story for a theme anthology, I will work with the author—sometimes at length—in order to get the story to a point where it works for me. That doesn't always work out—sometimes a story just won't fit no matter what you do to it—but while I don't think a solicitation should mean automatic acceptance, I think an editor does owe it to a writer to go the extra mile editorially when a story is written to order. This is partially a necessity with anthologies, too, as the anthologist typically sells the anthology to the publisher with the promise of certain writers contributing, so if "Big Name Writer" turns in a subpar story, it behooves you to work with him to make it suitable since the publisher will likely be unhappy if you promised a story by him and then didn't deliver. Fortunately, most "big names" got to be big names because they're good at what they do.

Ellen Datlow: I currently edit invitation-only anthologies, but I worked for *OMNI Magazine* and online for 17 years and *SCIFICTION* for over 5 years.

As an editor skimming incoming mail I would most definitely look at cover letters mentioning respectable credits and put them aside to read myself. Everything else would go to a reader, who would read the slush and pass on the good manuscripts to me with a note as to what she liked about the story. But as far as my acceptance or rejection of a story—credits mean nothing. It's the story itself. I bought a few first stories by writers I'd never heard of before (at least a couple passed on to me by my slush reader). In one case it was at *OMNI* and although my reader knew the story was wrong for *OMNI*, he passed it on to me because he knew I was reading for an original anthology and that the story might work for that. It did, and I bought it.

Also at *OMNI* I commissioned several series of thematic short-shorts. By commissioning them I mean actually promising I'd buy these short shorts from writers I'd mostly worked with or at least trusted to hand in what I needed because I'd have to pay a kill fee if I didn't take the story. I commissioned a story by a writer whose novels I loved and hadn't realized till he told me that it was the first story he'd ever written.

So it's really a question of getting on an editor's radar one way or another.

Mike Resnick: None. I judge the story, not what the author did for some other editor in the past.

Stanley Schmidt: Prior credits have no effect on my decision to accept or reject.

Gorgon Van Gelder: Almost none. When I get a submission, the question facing me is, is this a story that readers of F&SF will like? A list of publishing credits doesn't do much to answer that question.

Michael Knost: What are the first things you look for in a story?

John Joseph Adams: The first thing that usually grabs me is voice; if the story has a good narrative voice, that's the easiest way to make it stand out from the rest of the pack in the slush pile.

Ellen Datlow: I don't exactly "look" for anything. I read every submission (whether slush or something I've requested) with the hopes of being enveloped by the story and swept away by the storytelling.

Of course, the story also needs to fit the theme of the anthology for which it's submitted. And that it goes well with and doesn't duplicate earlier stories I've already bought for the anthology.

James Patrick Kelly: Does it fit our theme?

Mike Resnick: Accessibility. Is it easy to continue from one line to the next... because it's my job to read it, and if *I* find it difficult, why should the reader, who isn't being paid to read it, bother with it?

Stanley Schmidt: I start reading a story at the slow speed I use for things I'm interested in, and then try to shift to the much higher speed I use to look for anything that interests me enough to warrant spending serious time on the story. If it draws me in and makes me keep reading slowly, it has a good chance of being accepted. If it lets me shift to speed-reading, it probably doesn't—unless something (like a fascinating new idea) catches my eye and makes me slow back down.

Gordon Van Gelder: An assured narrative voice is probably #1 on the list, followed by some sort of STORY (as opposed to too many submissions I receive that don't seem to have an actual tale to tell).

Michael Knost: What are the most common reasons you reject manuscripts?

SHORT FICTION: A ROUNDTABLE DISCUSSION
WITH SHORT STORY EDITORS

John Joseph Adams: It's not a very useful answer, but *they're just not interesting enough*. Sure, there are a fair number of stories that are just so poorly written that the story can be rejected before the editor even engages on a story level, but the majority of stories submitted are at least competently written on a line-by-line level; whether or not they have something to say is another matter. An editor's interest-level is like a slippery eel; writers too often approach short stories as if they have the luxury of a novel's pacing, but in a short story, every line has to count. Also, the form is not a forgiving one, so any missteps the writer makes tend to be magnified.

Ellen Datlow: The stories are boring and don't hold my attention.

The characters are behaving stupidly.

The dialog is clunky.

There's no story, just a bunch of scenes thrown together and tied up with a horrific, usually telegraphed-from-the-first-page climax (most common in bad horror).

Mike Resnick: Exceptionally poor writing on page 1 will do it. So will a thinly disguised retelling of a major novel (or, far more often, a successful TV show or movie).

Gordon Van Gelder: 1. Story feels like the same-ol', same-ol', without any spark to it.

2. Story is trying too hard to entertain.

3. Story is trying too hard to do other things and forgets that it's meant to entertain.

Michael Knost: When reading a manuscript, are you looking for a reason to accept it—or are you looking for a reason to reject it?

John Joseph Adams: That's not how I approach reading manuscripts, really. I mean, I want each story I read to be fantastic, and I try to go into reading each one with a completely open mind. Great stories are few and far between, so I'd hate to miss out on one because I didn't give it the proper attention, or went into it looking for a reason to reject it. There are stories that I read that I get a good feeling about early on, and as I'm reading it, I think I'll be accepting it, but plenty of those turn out to disappoint by the time I get to the end; so in those cases, I guess you could say I start looking for reasons to accept them, but it doesn't always work out. Ultimately, it's an intuitive process that's hard to explain, but like science fiction or pornography (to paraphrase Damon Knight and Justice Potter Stewart), you know a good story when you see it.

Ellen Datlow: Depends on whether I have too many stories coming in (for a magazine or an anthology) or too few. If I have too much coming in and a lot of good work but nothing great, it's easier to reject those that are less than excellent.

Mike Resnick: You always hope you're about to discover the next Bradbury or Willis, so of course you hope they give you a reason to fall in love with it. You start each story with no opinion and hopefully no preconception, and it's up to the story to please you or turn you off.

SHORT FICTION: A ROUNDTABLE DISCUSSION
WITH SHORT STORY EDITORS

Stanley Schmidt: I don't need a specific reason to reject a manuscript—that's what necessarily happens to at least 99% of all submissions, because I only have room for 1%. So what I'm looking for is a reason to buy, which will be some combination of good writing and good ideas. I suppose another way to say that is that my commonest reason for rejecting a story is that I don't see anything in it special enough to make it stand out from 99% of the competition.

Gordon Van Gelder: I try not to read submissions unless I'm in a state of mind where I'm looking to be entertained. I also try not to read submissions when I'm hurried.

Michael Knost: Hypothetically speaking, if you have room for just one remaining story in your magazine/anthology, and you have two excellent tales to choose from, how do you make your decision?

John Joseph Adams: If they're both truly excellent, I would circumvent your question by appealing to the publisher to allow for some word count expansion so that both could be included. For most anthologies, that shouldn't be a problem, and for magazines, since they're ongoing, it shouldn't be a problem either. If I was somehow locked into making such a decision, however, I suppose I would probably weigh each author's potential fan bases, to see which one being in the anthology might benefit the book more (assuming the stories are equally awesome, as your question seems to suggest).

Ellen Datlow: If it's a magazine I would ask the writer to let me hang on to the story for a few months. During that time, if I can't get it out of my head, I'll buy it anyway.

For an anthology, if one story is more unusual and seems to fit a "hole" in the anthology, I might take that one. If they're both equally fantastic I'll ask my in-house editor if we can squeeze it in.

James Patrick Kelly: Is the table of contents balanced? How well does the story fit the theme of the anthology?

Mike Resnick: The easy way, of course, is to choose the length that fits. I assume that's not a consideration for this question. I'd say you choose for balance. If you're top-heavy on downbeat stories or fantasy or military, select the opposite. (Good thing you said it was anthology. Otherwise you buy them both and run one in the following issue.)

Stanley Schmidt: If I have two excellent stories to choose from, the deciding factor may be which is most different from others that I already have in the works. Or, if one still needs lots of editing and the other doesn't, I'll go with the one that doesn't—which should give writers an incentive to make sure every submission is in as polished a form as they can make it.

Gordon Van Gelder: I'm sorry to put it this way, but your hypothetical case doesn't have much bearing on reality. For one thing, excellent stories don't come along every day. Or every week. There are plenty of good stories around, but truly excellent ones are rare. For another thing, if I'm assembling a magazine and I've only got room for one story, I'm doing something wrong, because that means I have no inventory. Anthologies are different, more finite (in the sense that there's usually a word-count limit), and if I were in the position of having to choose between two stories for an anthology, I'd base my decision on which story fits the book best—which one complements the other stories better, which one addresses the theme of the book better.

But again, when an editor is faced with a choice like the one you posit, it's rarely a matter of choosing between two excellent works. I mean, if I'd been editing *Welcome to the Greenhouse* and I'd suddenly been stuck with two excellent stories at the last minute, I would have tried to buy them both and then, if need be, squeeze out a lesser story.

Michael Knost: What influence, if any, does author name recognition have with regards to acquiring or rejecting stories?

John Joseph Adams: Name recognition might cause me to invite an author to submit a story, but it would still have to be just as good as anything else for me to accept it. If I'm on the fence as to whether or not to accept something, name recognition might serve as a tie-breaker.

And as for rejecting stories, I would never reject something due to name recognition; in that case, I assume we're talking about a writer who has submitted a ton of stuff, none of which has worked for me. Even in those cases, I always try to approach each story with an open mind. I can think of at least one instance in which I bought a story by a writer after I had rejected several dozen stories, and there have been other times where I may not have bought the story but at least was impressed by it despite the writer's repeated previous attempts that didn't hit the mark.

Ellen Datlow: If a really big name writes me an original story, I'll hope very hard that it's wonderful and that I'll love it. Because you need names to sell an anthology (now more than ever).

But if I'm sent a brilliant story by an unknown, I'll of course buy it. You need to balance every anthology you edit. Putting together an anthology of all unknown writers will doom the anthology to oblivion, and it'll be very difficult to get a book contract again.

Anthology editing and magazine editing is *always* a balancing act of creating the best issue or anthology you can that will sell.

Publishing is a business. Publishers that make no money will not stay in business. Editors whose magazines or anthologies sell no copies will not be in the business for long.

James Patrick Kelly: Large, but not decisive.

Mike Resnick: You want Names on the cover of the magazine or anthology; it would be ridiculous to claim otherwise. But you want stories that are worthy of those names, and if the authors don't supply them, as painful as it is to both sides, you reject them or at least return them with specific suggestions for rewrites.

Stanley Schmidt: Author name, like prior credits, has no effect on my decision. An advantage of editing a magazine is that I can afford to take a chance on something unusual, but my magazine's success depends on its readers trusting it to provide material they really like most of the time. Nobody is at his or her best all the time, and while publishing a big name on a substandard story may give newsstand sales a little boost for one issue, ultimately it undermines the trust we depend on to keep readers coming back. So I'd rather publish a knockout story by a complete unknown than a so-so story by the biggest name in the business.

Gordon Van Gelder: I've never worked in a bookstore, but I doubt many customers come in and ask, "Give me the new book by someone I've never heard of before." Consumers look for certain writers' names, and consequently, so do I. If I see "S. King" or "C. Willis" or "K. Wilhelm" on the return address of an envelope, I'm going to grab that story before I grab the one by "John Q. Public." But I'm also going to read that story with a different set of expectations than I would read a story from a stranger—after all, if I'm reading a new story by, say, Ted Sturgeon, I can't make myself forget that this is the writer who gave the world "Baby Is Three." So the short answer to your question is, name recognition has a lot of influence, but it varies from name to name.

Michael Knost: How much editorial give-and-take do you see on the average purchased story?

John Joseph Adams: Editing short stories is kind of a buyer's market, so editors can generally reject stories that are good but don't quite work; as a result, I'll generally just accept stories that I'm happy to run as-is, and will just make suggestions to the author that they are free to take or discard as they see fit. If there are any changes that absolutely must be made in order for me to publish a story, before accepting it, I will make suggestions to the author and ask them to revise and resubmit. But to answer your question: on average, not much give-and-take; I do a close line edit on every story I buy, but only very occasionally do I do a heavy edit on story that requires extensive revision.

Ellen Datlow: I can count the number of times that I've published a story with no editing on one hand—and that's in 30 years of short story editing. So there's almost always give and take before a story I buy and edit sees print.

Mike Resnick: Almost none. My anthologies, with two exceptions, have been by invitation only, and I okay the idea before the author sits down to write it. And on a magazine, there are so many hundreds of submissions per issue, that I can always find what I need without arguing a writer into going back to the drawing board and giving me what I want (though very occasionally I'll do so; I do it much more on anthologies, since those are pre-sold stories, and rejection is an absolute last resort).

Stanley Schmidt: There's a fair but highly variable amount of give-and-take on the stories we publish. I don't rewrite stories I've bought; my philosophy is to buy stories I like and then print them. If I don't like a story quite enough to do that, I'll tell the writer why and challenge him or her to come up with changes that make us both like it better.

Gordon Van Gelder: On the average story, I send the author about

a dozen or two dozen suggestions, mostly of the line-editing sort. But I don't usually send a contract to an author unless I'm willing to publish the story as is. Two or three times a month, I'll reject a story with suggestions and I'll invite the writer to send me a revised version of the story. Those stories sometimes take two or three passes before I either accept them or pass on them.

Michael Knost: As a follow up, how often do you accept a story that needs no improvements/adjustments?

John Joseph Adams: Rarely does a story need no editing at all; even those that are basically perfect as submitted, generally can use a line edit here or there.

Ellen Datlow: Most stories I accept (or plan to accept) need improvements, from the very minor to major rewrites.

If I love a story and there are only some minor edits, I'll accept and pay for the story and then work on it with the writer.

But any heavy rewriting required goes on before a story is ever accepted by me. I will tell the writer in advance that I think the story needs work, here are my notes. I'll further say that if he's willing to work with me I can't guarantee that I'll buy the story, but I'd very much like to see a rewrite and if he can pull it off I'll probably buy the story.

Mike Resnick: By the time I buy it, it usually needs only a light line-edit, if that. There are too many good stories out there to buy one that I personally have to spend hours fixing.

Stanley Schmidt: A few stories require no changes at all; many require a few minor corrections or clarifications; some go through two or three significant revisions after I first see them.

Gordon Van Gelder: A story that "needs" no changes? I accept them all the time. How often do I accept a story that "couldn't benefit" from a change or three? Rarely. But F&SF is lucky enough to have contributors like Albert Cowdrey, Ursula K. Le Guin, Robert Silverberg, Kate Wilhelm, and Gene Wolfe who excel at the writing craft and we get plenty of stories that could easily run as-is.

Michael Knost: What elements of the craft do you see most beginners and up-and-comers struggling with?

John Joseph Adams: Style, structure, and voice are the hardest things to master. It just takes some time and practice reading critically, so that the writer can learn to deconstruct the stories to discover what makes them work (or not).

Ellen Datlow: Establishing their own voice.

Mike Resnick: Narrative hooks, characterization, and accessibility of their prose.

Stanley Schmidt: Surprisingly many writers (even experienced ones!) have trouble with basic principles of English, like accurate word use and punctuation. Others don't realize that good writing isn't enough—to satisfy readers in this field, you also have to have something new and interesting to say.

Gordon Van Gelder: It's hard to give you a general answer to that question because it varies so much from one writer to another—one might have trouble with characterizations, another with infodumping, and a third with pacing. You can take any good basic writing guide like Damon Knight's or Barry Longyear's and go through it chapter by chapter; for every chapter subject (like plot, setting, or dialogue) and you'll find some writers are struggling with it while other writers have an innate grasp of how it works.

Michael Knost: What advice would you offer a serious beginner/up-and-comer? What would you suggest they do to improve their craft?

John Joseph Adams: I always say that the best thing a writer can do is probably read slush. It's really illuminating to put yourself in that position, where you have to evaluate a stack of manuscripts in a short period of time—it really allows you to see how cut-throat an editor has to be when deciding what to buy. The lessons you'll learn won't be immediately obvious—and may even be hard to put into words—but I think you just can't help but learn a lot from the process, even if it's just stuff you sort of absorb without realizing it. In the past, it might have been difficult to get such a gig, but these days, if you're willing to volunteer your time, opportunities for reading slush are plentiful, as magazines like *Lightspeed* and *Fantasy* use teams of volunteers to help manage the workload. Other magazines do that as well, and there are a huge number of markets out there right now that one could potentially read slush for.

Ellen Datlow: Write as much as they can and experiment in style, voice, tone, point of view, and genre. That's why short stories are the best type of fiction to begin with. Write one story. Go back and rewrite it. Once you submit it start that next immediately.

Read everything. Use everything around you for fodder. Never throw out failed stories; you might be able to cannibalize them for another story or novel in the future.

Try to figure out what it is about specific writers whose work you admire that gets to you. For example, Elmore Leonard writes great dialog.

There are writers who somehow manage to pull off amazing feats—they make hideous characters memorable in a good way (Hannibal Lector). How does Harris do it?

What are the different ways good writers draw the reader into a story?

James Patrick Kelly: Write until your fingers bleed. Show your work to other people in a rigorous workshop like Clarion or Viable Paradise.

Mike Resnick: Just write as much as you can and read as much as you can. If you plan to attend workshops, be very selective of your instructors. Not to denigrate any others, but the two that seem to produce the most successful writers year in and year out are Clarion and Writers of the Future.

Stanley Schmidt: Do your research—on at least two levels. First, research your story, making sure that it's built on a solid foundation, with any checkable facts checked and correct and the background, characters, and action thoroughly and consistently developed. Second, research your potential markets. This is especially important now that more markets are accepting electronic submissions. Since we started accepting them, I've seen a big increase in submissions from writers who apparently have no idea what we do and haven't bothered to try to find out. My impression is that they figure since it no longer costs money to submit a story, they might as well submit everything everywhere. I often tell writers that if they think there's the slightest chance their story might be right for my magazine, they should let me decide. That presupposes they've learned enough about the magazine to have some idea what might be right for it. Some things are completely inappropriate for any particular market, and no editor appreciates having his or her time wasted with those. So I'd advise writers to familiarize themselves with any market they plan to submit to, not with the idea of imitating it (nobody wants to publish next year what they were publishing last year), but to get a feel for what might or might not work there.

Gordon Van Gelder: My first piece of advice might simply be a reaction to your use of the word "serious," but it's this: write to entertain! I've seen a few writers who were so preoccupied with their ambitions and their drive to impress that they didn't find their voice until someone told them, "Relax. Just tell us an interesting story."

Piece of advice #2: when *Light* came out, M. John Harrison made a great comment about his own writing that "If you steal a milk truck, you can't complain that the vehicle doesn't handle like a Ferrari." I think it's great for writers if they try driving both milk trucks and Ferraris and learn what both do well. That is, it's good to try different sorts of stories and different approaches. Charles Coleman Finlay told me that in every story he sent me, he was testing out some new aspect of his craft. Sometimes his tests worked, sometimes they didn't, but he learned from every one of them.Taking an approach like that is one of the best suggestions I can make.

LONG FICTION:
A ROUNDTABLE DISCUSSION WITH NOVEL EDITORS

MODERATED BY MAX MILLER

Max Miller is a freelance writer who has written for several magazines and newspapers. His day job as a biology teacher often keeps him too busy to write, but also offers endless ideas to explore ... not to mention hundreds of characters and emotions. He is currently wrestling with a novel.

Ginjer Buchanan is Editor-in-Chief at Ace Books and Roc Books, the two science fiction and fantasy imprints of Penguin Group (USA); she has worked at Ace since 1984, and has been nominated for both the Hugo Award and the World Fantasy Award for her editing. She was a Guest of Honor at OryCon in 2008, Foolscap in 2000, and ArmadilloCon in 1988, and was Toastmaster at the World Fantasy Convention in 1989.

Peter Crowther is the recipient of numerous awards for his writing, his editing, and as publisher, for the hugely successful PS Publishing (now including the Stanza Press poetry subsidiary and PS Artbooks, a specialist imprint dedicated to the comics field).

Jason Sizemore is a writer and editor based in Lexington, Kentucky. He is the editor and publisher of Apex Books, as well as *Apex Digest*, a quarterly science fiction and horror digest. As a writer he has published several stories in genre magazines.

Jo Fletcher is founder and publisher of Jo Fletcher Books. She spent years in Fleet Street as an investigative reporter, then critic, and is an award-winning poet and writer. She has won both the World Fantasy Award and the British Fantasy Karl Edward Wagner Award for her work within the genre.

Nick Mamatas is a horror, science fiction, and fantasy author and editor for the Haikasoru line of translated Japanese science fiction novels for Viz Media. His fiction has been nominated for several awards, including several Bram Stoker Awards, while he has also been recognized for his editorial work with a Bram Stoker Award, as well as World Fantasy Award and Hugo Award nominations.

Lou Anders is the Hugo Award-winning editorial director of the SF&F imprint Pyr, a Chesley Award-winning art director, and the editor of nine anthologies. He has also been nominated for five additional Hugos, four additional Chesleys, as well as the Philip K. Dick, Locus, Shirley

Jackson, and three WFC Awards. Visit him online at www. louanders.com, on Twitter @LouAnders, and on Facebook.

From an early age, **Amanda DeBord** found herself torn between two loves: the love of horror, and the love of criticism. These fires were stoked by a constant stream of subpar ghost stories aimed at children ("The Ghost at Dawn's House? Did anyone actually fall for that?"), and she has since been able to funnel her energies into a career protecting the world from lambs in wolves clothing. She resides in Lexington, Kentucky, with her husband and two cats, and when she's not crushing dreams with her red pen, she's tearing up the roller derby flat track as Sugar Shock from the Rollergirls of Central Kentucky (ROCK). She is currently the senior editor for Seventh Star Press and also edits for Sideshow Press and anyone else who wants an honest opinion.

Max Miller: Are you looking for great authors or a great work?

Ginjer Buchanan: Both. In fantasy, it does seem that the readers expect trilogies or series. So if we are seriously considering a submission of that nature, we will ask if there is more to the story. In science fiction, the continuing character, or cast of characters, does not seem to be as important to the reader.

Peter Crowther: Great work. Always. Publishers should be selling books, not people and not reputations. It's all too often that we see someone whom we considered to be a truly great writer turn in a weak piece of work. That also goes for musicians and, to a degree, artists. So it's the book that counts. And the painting. And the song. Think of Paul McCartney: Hard to imagine the man who wrote *Blackbird, Eleanore Rigby* and *Yesterday* could also turn out *Mull of Kintyre, Ebony and Ivory,* and *Someone's Knocking at the Door.* So, if those were books, then I'd publish the first three without a second's hesitation. But I wouldn't touch the last three with a bargepole.

Jason Sizemore: I see having a great novel as part of being a great author. As a small press publisher, I need to know that the author is somebody who is friendly, can handle the stress of the business, a professional, has basic Internet marketing skills, and doesn't mind a little self-promotion. The small press is a great platform for getting noticed, having your more esoteric works published, or even seeing your first novel in print, but to be successful the author-publisher dynamic has to be strong.

Jo Fletcher: On the whole I would have to say great authors, because that's the best way to solid sales. If you have a great work, you may sell shedloads of it, but that's that: It's a one-time event. You may repackage and find more readers that way, but there will be nothing else for everyone who's already bought and loved it to read next. And if a reader loves a book, they tend to want more—I know I do. If I find a new author that I love, I then go back and buy everything else that author's written—or if it's a new writer, I wait impatiently for each new book as it comes out.... That's why, when a bestselling author dies, publishers do from time to time look to continue with a different author (not that that is always as successful as one might hope). So of course I would have published *Gone with the Wind,* but I would always have been hoping Margaret Mitchell would write the sequel!

Nick Mamatas: Both, of course. I don't know if anyone wishes to publish the product of a good author's bad day or mere contractual obligation.

Lou Anders: I'm not sure what the distinction is. An author is great because they produce great work. I am looking for work that excites me and thrills me, work that has me leaping out my chair to run tell my wife about it, or forcing me to reluctantly take a break from the manuscript to look up and take a moment to breath. I acquire manuscripts that I am passionate about. If I am not passionate about it, I don't acquire it. On that, I'm always surprised by people who try to argue an editor out of a rejection. If an editor isn't passionate about a project, you don't want them as your editor. Editors are the number one advocate that a book has, both externally and *internally*. We are a company of around fifty people and only two or three of us will have read the manuscript. All the various departments—sales, marketing, production, rights, art—need to be reminded what kind of a book this is, why it matters, what's exciting about it, and why they should care. The editor is the book's cheerleader internally. If an editor doesn't care about a book, no one else will. (I should say that my authors are all great people as well as great authors, and many of those that I have gotten to know personally through working with them and hanging out at conventions have gone on to become dear friends. But it is great work that drew me to them.)

Amanda DeBord: While I'd like to think it's as easy as "Great authors produce great work," it's not. I'm looking for great work, and I don't care who you are. Think of your favorite "great author."

Surely he or she has some pieces that are better than others. I think every writer has that one piece that makes him say to himself, "Wow. Where did that come from, and why can't I do it every time?" I believe in skill, in hard work, practice, and good editing. But I also believe that there is a spirit of art that can inhabit a piece and make it something very, very special. Great authors are better at calling up this spirit, and produce those great works more consistently, but in my experience, it's the work itself that moves people, not the name on the cover.

Max Miller: How important is it for an author to prove his or her marketing ability before you are willing to make an offer? i.e., book signings, appearances, etc.?

Ginjer Buchanan: Not at all.

Peter Crowther: Not important at all ... save that we expect our authors to sign tip sheets and, of course, we hope they'll use all the available media to advertise any product of ours that features their work. After all, it's a two-way deal, this publishing lark. Writers expect to see promotion from their publisher and that's absolutely right and proper. But publishers need reciprocation.

Jason Sizemore: If an author shows no desire to assist in the promotion of their title, then I will not make an offer. In my case, I don't have the resources to employ a marketing division that will help beat the bushes for sales (nor do most other small publishers).

What I can do is make sure your book gets seen by the major trade journals, line up interviews and features, have your book reviewed.... and occasionally buy advertising. When I sign an author I hope that they'll do things like convention appearances, initiate their own publicity via newspapers and blogs, and be a positive force on the Internet. Not all these are required, but I do like to see a little effort.

Jo Fletcher: Absolutely not at all. I'm taking on the writing ability, not the person's ability to market his or herself. These days email and the Interweb make it much easier for us to work with authors in different countries, for example, but in the past probably the most you could expect to be able to do with someone in America or the Antipodes was to get some signed book plates or to do a telephone interview or two—and that never stopped anyone publishing foreign authors. My colleagues in the Maclehose Press publish mostly authors in translation, and I am willing to bet a lot of them speak little or no English, making interviews and signings pretty hard. That doesn't stop those books selling. I have never turned down a book I loved because the author doesn't want to do anything publicity-related.

I won't say it isn't terrific when an author does help—and, of course, we do tell everyone what we'd hope from them ideally—these days, we like them to have a website, to Tweet if possible, and to blog—even if it's just writing the occasional blog for the JFB site. Of course it helps, and I would certainly try and persuade a new author to be prepared to do some sort of publicity, but signings are generally not as important now as they used to be—there are far fewer book signings these days because (for reasons that escape me) they don't attract the audiences they used to. I have had authors who don't want anything to do with the publicity; they just write the books—in those cases we can try to use the enigma factor to garner a bit of extra attention! Of course, it's sometimes frustrating if they don't wish to (or cannot) do anything more to help with publicity, but it's not the end of the world.

Nick Mamatas: At Haikasoru, we almost exclusively publish work in translation, so the authors are generally not available to or capable of independently marketing their work here in the US. So we're interested in excellent concepts, good writing, and work that is "culturally translatable." When authors are available—Tow Ubukata made an appearance at New York Comic-Con when the *Murdock Scramble* anime premiered, and hyped the forthcoming translation of the novel version while there—it's great.

Lou Anders: No one is required to "prove their marketing ability." We have a marvelous publicity and marketing department already. However, in this day and age, it's certainly recommended that authors maintain a presence on Facebook and Twitter, etc... and I encourage all authors, and all wanna-be authors, to have a web presence. For one thing, when I hear about an up-and-coming author that I am curious about, the first thing I do is go to their website to see if I can find either an interview with them or a short fiction sample. You need to be searchable and findable. You never know who is looking.

Amanda DeBord: Usually, when we get a manuscript, it's from someone who already knows about us and knows how we do things. They also know that we don't (yet!) have a large marketing machine behind us, and that if they want to be successful, they're going to have to put in some legwork. Before we accept a manuscript, we take a good look at the author to see if they've got the professionalism and drive to make it work. That said, when I read something that really moves me, that I really feel passionate about, I want the entire world to experience it RIGHT NOW. It's easy for me because I'm just the editor, but I want to take authors by their shoulders sometimes and shake them and say, "You've done something amazing here! Where are the skywriters? Where are the full-page *New York Times* ads?"

Max Miller: What influence, if any, do cover page publishing credits have in regard to your decision of acceptance or rejection?

Ginjer Buchanan: If someone has had a body of short fiction published and thus is known or has attended certain writers' workshops, it's good information to have. But the work is the work—and not everybody who writes terrific short stories can write to length (and vice versa).

Peter Crowther: A writer's "currency" (for want of a better word) is, of course, very helpful to selling copies of books ... even though, as I said in my answer to your first question, just because a writer has produced one or more fabulous books it doesn't necessarily follow that their next book will be equally great. But accepting this obvious potential aid to the income stream, I would have no hesitation in bouncing something by, say, a household name if it didn't rock my boat. Similarly, I have no hesitation in accepting a first work by someone who nobody has ever heard of if it's an excellent book. What we need to remember is that the punter will soon spot when a publisher is given to bullshitting obviously inferior works by so-called household names ... and once you lose the public's trust then you may as well just pack up shop and go home.

Jason Sizemore: Near zero influence. If I see that the author has recently won the Writers of the Future contest or had a novel published by a larger house like Tor, I'll give the story or manuscript a few extra hundred words to catch my interest. Otherwise, I'm indifferent to your credits.

Jo Fletcher: If you mean what the person has written before, not much. The only things that are important to me are: 1. Is it a great book, and 2. Do I think I can sell it, and 3. Can I see a long-term relationship with this author? I can even live without number 3 if 1 and 2 are spot-on.

Does it help if someone's written short fiction? Yes, of course it does: with any luck it will have taught them how to write, or at least improved their writing, and it might even have built them a fan base. But is it a prerequisite to getting published? Absolutely not.

Lou Anders: Very little. While short fiction credits are nice, they don't translate into novel sales. Also, short story writing and novel writing are different skills. In some cases, I think that they are actually antithetical.

Amanda DeBord: None at all. I know a lot of small presses are trying to build their brands, and there is great capital that comes along from being able to say that someone else believed in this author, too. I suppose that helps. But if it's a great story, it's a great story. I'm never going to turn away something awesome just because no one has taken a chance on it yet.

Max Miller: What are the first things you look for in a story?

Ginjer Buchanan: A strong beginning and a strong ending.

Jo Crowther: I'm a sucker for great opening lines. That's the first thing. Among others (notably Elmore Leonard and Stephen King) Tim Lebbon is a genius at this. The one I always use as an example (and I don't have it in front of me so I'm paraphrasing) is the opening sentence of Tim's *The First Law*. It goes thus: "They had been adrift for five days before they first saw the island." Superb. So many questions—i.e. so many reasons to read on. Who are 'they'? What's happened to them that they're now adrift? And what about this island? (Face it, there's no way the island is a good thing ... so right from the get-go you're secretly saying *don't go to the island!*)

After that, it's just the simple (hah!) art of storytelling. Some people can do it and others can't. I use the analogy of a musician. You can teach someone to play the piano, but you can't teach them to write something like *Yesterday* (to hark back to one of my earlier answers). The same goes with storytelling. You can teach someone the rudiments of language, but you can't teach them to write *The Stand* or *Something Wicked This Way Comes*. There are those who would argue with that, but that's the way I see it.

Jason Sizemore: I like an engaging plot that doesn't take too long to get moving. I'm the furthest thing from a poet, but I like prose that has a discernible rhythm or style. I'm also a sucker for character-driven plots.

Finally, does the conclusion make sense in terms of the story? So many good stories are ruined by a weak ending.

Jo Fletcher: Spelling. Plot. Characterisation. Good writing. Unputdownability ...

Nick Mamatas: Concept: I don't want to do three military SF novels in the same season, or three time travel novels. Then, POV—first or third person, that tells me a lot about the story right before anything else.

Lou Anders: Narrative drive. The quality of writing that makes you want to keep the pages turning. The truth is, you can tell in a page or two, sometimes even a paragraph, if an author can write. If it isn't present from the get-go, it doesn't emerge later. You either have it or you don't. That being said, editors are all individuals and have their own tastes. What floats one editor's boat doesn't necessarily float another's. I recommend that beginning authors read the Books Sold column in *Locus* magazine. *Locus* has a monthly report that details who sold what via which agent to what editor at which imprint. It is a wonderful resource for learning not only what is currently selling but also what respective editor's tastes and specialties are.

Amanda DeBord: I look for a story that I care about. Technical problems can be fixed. But if I have no reason to keep turning the page, a reader won't either. I know a lot of readers who are stubborn and will finish any book they buy, but you can be sure they won't buy a second one from that author. There are a lot of stories out there that are neat ideas, or cool characters or creative details. But if I'm not concerned over what happens to the characters, it's not for me.

Max Miller: What are the most common reasons you reject manuscripts?

Ginjer Buchanan: Lack of originality. We do get really badly written stuff, of course, but mostly we get adequately-written-but-nothing-new-to-say manuscripts.

Peter Crowther: Because they fail all the points I just made in the last answer. Sometimes the presentation leaves something to be desired, but generally, I tend to make allowances for that. Most often (but by no means always), I'll know whether I'm going to like a piece or not within the first half-dozen pages. If I like it at that stage then it's a 20/80 chance I'll still like it at the end (20 being, yes, I *will* like it). Based on the amount of manuscripts we've been receiving in the past (we're now not considering unsolicited material, incidentally), the ratio when I start reading is lower than 1/99.

Jason Sizemore: Frankly, a good 80% are poorly written. If you can't get your verb tenses correct in your opening paragraph, that doesn't give me much hope for the rest of the story or novel.

After that, most people fall into the rejection pile for not following the guidelines. I've never been harsh enforcing our guidelines to the letter, but if we don't accept post-mailed submissions, don't send them. If you're sending something without a speculative angle, don't bother. The guidelines are supposed to help you, not hurt you.

Jo Fletcher: I suppose the biggest reason for me is bad writing. I can fix things like grammar if the plot and characterisation are there, but I have plenty of choice of great books to publish, so I don't need to take something that might have a grain of hope but needs completely rewriting—apart from anything else, I simply don't have the time. I'm not looking for a rip-off or mash-up of the last bestseller, either, and telling me how much better you are than (fill in name of bestseller of choice here) doesn't help either.

Nick Mamatas: We're a small list; ten to twelve books a year. "No more room right now" is sufficient. Of course, all our submissions have previously been published in Japan, so all are of publishable quality.

Lou Anders: Boredom. Disinterest. No passion for the material. The slow, mountain realization that I am reading further out of obligation to an agent I respect, guilt that it's been in my inbox too long, or because my arm has been twisted by a colleague, or just to satisfy some notion of due diligence, but that I have no love for the material and consequently no intention of actually buying it. The minute I realize it's not for me, I stop. My inbox is too large and my time too short.

Amanda DeBord: There are probably two main reasons I'll reject a manuscript. One is easy to fix, the other one not so much. The first one is technical. Can you write a coherent sentence? You'd be surprised at the abominations of English I see sometimes. I think people read, and think they know how words and grammar work, but they really don't. Either that, or they think they're Faulkner, and the rules don't apply to them. Having your own voice and your own style is very important, but if you don't know the way words work together, you're just going to distract your reader. The second problem is a lot harder to fix—it's just a story with nothing to say. Either it's a story that's been told a thousand times, or sometimes it's not even a story at all, just some neat people (or what the author thinks are neat people) saying or doing neat things. Sadly, we're not publishing magazine articles about people with interesting lives—we're publishing stories. Give it the campfire test. If you were sitting around with your buddies, would you tell them about your story? How would you tell it to get their attention? If you approach your story like you're sitting with your friends, you'll be doing all of your readers (and your editors!) a big favor.

Max Miller: When reading a manuscript, are you looking for a reason to accept it, or are you looking for a reason to reject it?

Ginjer Buchanan: A reason to reject. The smart writer will not provide me with one!

Peter Crowther: Well, both, I suppose. I don't set out to do one or the other. I just wait until that little voice in the back of my head says, *hey, this is good, isn't it!* or, more usually, *hey, this is one of the* *biggest turkeys we've ever been sent, isn't it!* And when I hear one of those voices then I either send it along to my assistant or I bounce it ... but always as gently and positively as possible. And I always bear in mind that I'm bouncing a piece of work and not a writer. The fact that the piece I've just read by that writer stinks to high heaven does not mean the next piece the writer sends me will be as bad. No indeedy ... that next piece could be *The Stand*.

Jason Sizemore: Generally, if I've made it past the first 2000 words, that means

1. I have a general grasp of your plot.
2. I believe the plot has potential.
3. Your writing style is up to professional levels.
4. You have a solid grasp of the English language.

It also means I'm looking for reasons to accept the story. Prior to the first 2000 words, I'm looking for reasons to reject you.

Jo Fletcher: I'm always hoping I'll love it. There are few things more exciting than finding a new author!

Nick Mamatas: We read sample chapters, not whole manuscripts, as it is not economical to translate an entire book before acquiring it. We look for both reasons to accept and to reject!

Lou Anders: I am looking for brilliance. I am looking for A+s, not merely passing grades. In an increasingly crowded publishing landscape, competence isn't enough. To stand out in the crowd, your writing has to *stand out in the crowd*. I'm looking for the best work that

I can possibly acquire. We get hundreds of unsolicited submissions a month and publish only twenty to thirty a year. There is no reason to ever take anything but the best. Always remember, publishing is a business not a charity. My job is to provide my employers with those books that I think will bring them a return in their considerable investment, not to make writers out of hopefuls. It is wonderful, absolutely wonderful, to make a new writer's dream come true by offering them their first book contract, but if I don't believe 100% in the worth of the material then I am betraying the confidence that has been placed in me by my boss.

Amanda DeBord: I like to give authors the benefit of the doubt. Rejecting things is no fun for anyone. But I will have to say that I go into a manuscript expecting to reject it.

Max Miller: How much editorial give-and-take do you see on the average purchased novel? And on average, what percentage of a submitted novel needs improvements or adjustments?

Ginjer Buchanan: Depends on whether it is a newbie author or not. First-timers need more work. But if you have to spend a lot of time editing an author that you have been working with for a decade, then you are both doing something wrong. And if you mean how often do we get a first-time submission that is pretty much fine as is—almost never.

Jason Sizemore: On average, our editors and authors go back and forth four or five times. When it comes to plot points, we generally give authors what they want (unless it causes an egregious hole in the novel). Grammatically, we adhere strictly to house style with little leeway given to the author.

Jo Fletcher: If you mean how much rewriting will need to be done, that's like asking how long is a piece of string. I use Track Changes, and I know it can be very dispiriting to see every single page covered in red (or whatever colour my computer has assigned me). But often it can just mean using the author's words, but in a slightly different order, or changing double quotes to single, or dashes to N-dashes. It saves an awful lot of time if you look at how the publisher's books are set before you submit and change those things yourself: English publishers use single quotes, three spaced ellipses ... and spaced N-dashes – like this, while American publishers use double quotes, closed-up ellipses...and closed-up M-dashes—(which we do use, but for broken-off word, thought, speech or action, not for colon or parentheses). If you've got that wrong, it has to be changed – and instantly your script is covered in colour!

Every manuscript is completely different, but they all take work. No writer is perfect - and that goes especially and several times over for new writers.

Lou Anders: This varies wildly depending on the author and the manuscript. All manuscripts go through three rounds of editing— my edits, the copy editor's edits, and a final in-house proofing stage. Typos and other errors will be caught right up to the end, but the amount of structural change that a manuscript requires varies considerably case to case. I have over the years moved or removed chapters, asked for as much as a quarter of a book to be rewritten, and altered the species of a main character. But two things should be pointed out: First, the manuscript belongs to the author, not the editor or the publisher, and in the end, all suggestions are just that—suggestions—and it is up to the author whether to implement them or not. Two, as I indicated above, this is a buyer's market. Why take on a manuscript that you think has potential but is a mess when there is no guarantee that the writer can bring it up to a professional level when the next manuscript in the queue is a shining diamond of perfection? The take-away from this is that you should ensure your manuscript is absolutely as professional and final as you can before submitting it. There is a wonderful line that Robert De Niro speaks in the film Ronin that I have always taken as a rule of thumb in editing: "If there is any doubt, there's no doubt."

Amanda DeBord: I'm not sure what a lot of other editors do, and (as I'm sure the authors appreciate), we rarely get to see the raw versions. I read an article in The New York Review of Books about Raymond Carver, and how his editor cut his pieces by up to 70%! That said, it differs from novel to novel. You kind of have to figure out what the author is trying to do and work within that. Editing is a dance. I could turn you into Faulkner (that might be a slight exaggeration), but should I?

Max Miller: What elements of the craft do you see most beginners and up-and-comers struggling with?

Ginjer Buchanan: It varies. In general though, I think people don't know when their story actually starts. Particularly in fantasy, new authors tend to put their world-building entirely up front.

Peter Crowther: My big bugbear is people starting out as a writer by writing a BIG novel. Don't do it! Think of writing as carpentry and make your first project a simple jewelry box with a hinged lid. When you've perfected that, move along to something a little more demanding. Do not make your first project the construction of a 25-room turreted multiple-level Bates Motel-type house with gazebo, turrets, outhouses, stables, indoor pool, and so on.

After that, characterization is something many folks foul up. They change the basic tenets of a character just because they need that character to do or say something at a particular juncture when the fact is that that character would never do or say that thing.

Dialogue. Oh my goodness, people really fall down on this. My suggestion is you do something that I still do with everything I write. I read it aloud to myself ... or to Nicky. In that situation, you know immediately if the dialogue is right or not.

And finally, so many writers—particularly those working in the so-called horror area—fail to make the reader care about the characters. A lot of them are just spare bodies brought in from Central Casting to be dispatched in as unpleasant a way as possible. Well, if I don't care about that character then ... well, I don't care about him. And if they're all like that then it kind of follows that I don't care about the book.

Jason Sizemore: I can always point out a new author by their lack of basic grammar skills. Most people aren't grammar experts...

unless you've studied to become an editor, your grammar abilities will have holes. But with practice and experience, you learn the difference between 'effect' and 'affect', when to use 'who' and 'whom', and how to avoid dangling modifiers.

Beginners and up-and-comers also have problems with punctuation, dialog attribution, and paragraph breaks... though I know plenty of experienced writers who share those issues as well!

Jo Fletcher: Use of language: Grammar is no longer taught in most of our schools and too few would-be writers see any need to teach themselves. In fact, knowing the difference between its and it's - the former is the possessive form, the latter a contraction – can make a huge difference in the way I look at a book. Apostrophes are really not hard, but they seem to stump far too many people. If you can't see the difference between *who's* and *whose*, go and treat yourself to a decent grammar and start learning, It will pay dividends.

Nick Mamatas: In my prior life as an editor of short fiction, I saw endless elementary errors of point of view. POV shifts for no reason, no understanding of where to begin a first person story, a lot of stuff borrowed from television rather than being properly based on texts: those were the big ones.

Lou Anders: Voice. Finishing any manuscript, even a bad one, is a herculean work. Anyone who has gotten to the point where they've spent a year or more to bang out 100,000 words of prose deserves a hearty round of applause. But that means that any story that comes in the door probably has a beginning, a middle, and an end. Plots are a dime a dozen, as are ideas. Ideas don't sell stories.

Plots don't sell stories. Fancy prose doesn't sell stories. Characters do. Voice does. The ability to compel readers to turn the page. A writer can either make you care or they can't. Voice comes with time and lots of practice.

Amanda DeBord: Voice. It happens to the best of us. But most of us start writing because we read H.P. Lovecraft or Clive Barker and thought, "I can do that!" Then we try to write just like them. Two problems with that: One, no you can't. Two, they already did it. So many beginners, I can almost point to the book they're trying to sound like. It takes a lot of confidence to have your own voice, though.

Also, knowing how to make a plot. Beginning, middle, end. Conflict, resolution. Just because it's an interesting what-if doesn't make it a story. I wrote this fantabulous *Saw*-style slasher (before *Saw*, too!) story once. It was great! Gory, twisted, surprising ending. Then I had a teacher ask me, "Why are you telling me this?" It hurt, but he was right. It was a scene. Maybe even a well-written scene, but it wasn't a story.

Max Miller: What advice would you offer a serious beginner or up-and-comer? What would you suggest they do to improve their craft?

Ginjer Buchanan: Read. A lot, and outside of the genre you want to write in. Join a writers' group that has a couple of published writers in it (and I don't mean writers who have self-pubbed). Or find one or two beta readers who are published. Take a couple novels that you admire (or that have sold well) and deconstruct them, up to and including transcribing a chapter or two.

Whatever you are working on, finish it. The world is full of wanna-bes who "have an idea." Maybe attend a few workshops or conferences. The craft *can* be taught—and you might find a session at one of them that will make a big difference to your work.

Peter Crowther: Read more and write more. They might say they read X pages and they write Y pages every damn day. *Well, good for you,* I'd say. And then I'd tell them once again, now read *more* and *write* more.

Jason Sizemore: If you have the innate ability to be a writer (and most people don't), then I offer three pieces of advice that should serve you well.

1. Read. A lot. Read in your genre. Outside your genre. Venture out and try modern literary classics. As a writer, there is much to be learned by reading Michael Chabon, Thomas Pynchon, Franz Kafka, Cormac McCarthy, or Mary Doria Russell.
2. Write. A lot. Write a daily blog. In a personal journal. Force yourself to do 500 words a day. If you're to become a master at a craft, you have to spend thousands of hours working on your craft.
3. Find a mentor. You'll need somebody to help you avoid the many minefields in this business.

Jo Fletcher: Write, read, write, read. And then do it all over again. Read as many different genres as you can, and as much non-fiction as fiction. I think a lot of the books written for children in the nineteenth century would stump many adult readers these days, and that's criminal. They say it takes 10,000 hours of practise to make an expert, and I reckon that's about right.

Nick Mamatas: Read widely. Read authors who aren't famous. You should be reading at least one book a week, every week, forever. Classics, avant-garde stuff, histories and biographies, the latest releases, small press stuff, superstars, genres you think you hate, anything and everything!

Amanda DeBord: Is there a writer who hasn't yet heard this? Write. Writewritewritewrite. All the damn time. Then find people who don't care about you to give you their honest opinion. Your friends will never ever help you in this regard. You think they're being honest, but they're not. I promise. Then do what they say. Even if you disagree with every part of you, save your manuscript, then try their suggestions on for size. I know that they don't understand what you were going for and their critiques demonstrate their ignorance. The thing is, your readers won't "know what you're going for" either, and you won't be there to stand behind them and fill in the blanks. Your work has to be able to stand on its own. One last one. It works better with short stories, but it's a great exercise. Cut your piece by 50%. Do a word count, then divide it in half and eliminate that many words. But they're good words! I know! Save the original with all your precious words, but just humor me and see what it looks like with the fat trimmed off. You'll be really surprised at how much fat there is, and I bet you'll find more than a few sentences that are better left off in the trash. If you've got a great little turn of phrase that you just have to show off, write it in your journal and use it sometime later.

Lou Anders: Get your 10,000 hours in as fast as you can. There is no way to improve other than by doing. Type "the end" on your first manuscript and move on to your second. Write the bad habits and the bad prose out of you as fast as you can, knowing that just like any other profession or craft, success comes with practice. Lots of it. Ambition does not equal ability. I may have all the ambition in the world to be a doctor, but if I have never been to med school you'd be a fool to make me your physician. People who think that writing doesn't require years to master are really insulting those writers who have put the time in to get where they are. Writing is a profession. Treat it like such. Write every day and know that success comes through hard work and long hours.

SEVENTH STAR PRESS

The home of
Science Fiction, Fantasy, and Horror.

Explore several authors of high quality speculative fiction in the Seventh Star Press catalog of novels, anthologies, single-author collections, and short stories, available in print and eBook formats. Seventh Star Press titles also feature a collection of genre artwork from several award-winning artists.

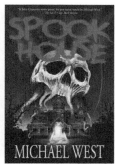

Connect with Seventh Star Press at:
www.seventhstarpress.com
seventhstarpress.blogspot.com
www.facebook.com/seventhstarpress

CPSIA information can be obtained at www.ICGtesting.com
Printed in the USA
LVOW012329070513

332780LV00010B/147/P